HEAVEN'S GONE TO HELL

Andrew J. Simpson

BareBackPress

This is a work of fiction. The characters, incidents, and dialogue are the products of the author's imagination and are not to be construed as real. Any resemblance to actual events or person, living or dead, is entirely coincidental.

BareBackPress
Hamilton, Ontario, Canada
For enquiries visit www.barebackpress.com
For information contact press@barebacklit.com
Cover art by Emma Jenkin Copyright © 2015
Author photo by Kaitlin Wainwright Copyright © 2014

STORIES

A Punch In The Face

LET'S SAY YOU'RE HAVING A BAD DAY. Let's say it's not just an ordinary bad day where you didn't get enough sleep, but one of those days that you really remember. Let's say you lost your wallet and you thought you knew where you'd left it, but you were wrong, or somebody stole it and you were parked on the street while you went and checked and somebody dinged your car and drove off without leaving a note.

You could have gotten fired that morning too, or diagnosed with cancer, but that might be too much and you've already got the point.

Now let's say you've got one of those expressions on your face – somewhere between I hate the world and I'm going to cry. A woman comes up to you in all this and she smiles and puts her hand on your arm and it doesn't feel bad really. It actually feels kind of nice. Let's say she doesn't stop there, though. Let's say she gives you a hug and leads you into the coffee shop down the street and buys you a coffee or a latte or a hot chocolate or whatever you want to drink, and then she buys you a cookie too.

Let's say this woman sits with you and she smiles at you some more and she tells you it'll be okay. I should add that this woman is a complete stranger, or she was five minutes ago.

Let's say it's at this point that you feel a stabbing pain in your lower abdomen. You gasp and she comes over beside you, and she hugs you and rubs your side and then she cradles your head and kisses the top of it.

Let's say you burst into tears, a little because you've had such a shitty day, but mostly because the pain isn't getting better, it's getting worse.

Let's say this woman says shh and tells you it'll be fine, better than fine, and she says you can rely on her and she'll make sure you're safe.

Imagine that when she says this you suddenly can't breathe and you think maybe it's an asthma attack, except that you've never had an asthma attack before. Let's say that you clutch her arm so tightly that she cries out, and you sputter 911, and then fall out of your chair.

Let's say this woman is truly kind. Let's say she calls 911 and she asks the coffee shop if anyone is a doctor or knows first aid or CPR or anything and then she gets down on the floor with her legs crossed and puts your head in her lap.

Let's say the ambulance is quick, because they were nearby or because the dispatch operator could hear the desperation in the woman's voice. Let's say the ambulance only takes four minutes, but that's still too slow. Let's say you've already asphyxiated and your heart stops right when the paramedics come through the door with the stretcher, and the paramedics can't get your heart started again and they can't get you to breathe again.

Now let's say that the afterlife is generally dull, and a really shitty day aside things were better when you were alive. Let's say also that people in the afterlife talk about this woman who was with you when you died, and what happened between you and this woman happens pretty regularly with her. She's so kind that she kills people.

Let's say time goes by. Years and years and one day you run into this woman, who was a serial killer, at least one a week for the last twenty years. Let's say this woman smiles at you and you wonder if she remembers you and you wonder if she knows she's a serial killer. One a week for twenty years is a lot, but maybe she never connected the dots.

The question is, when you meet this woman and she smiles at you, do you smile back and keep walking, or do you stop and tell her that she killed at least a thousand people over the last twenty years with kindness, or do you punch her in the face?

The Same Don River

ROBIN CREATED AN ALTERNATE UNIVERSE exactly like this one so that she could test the Butterfly Effect. The Robin in this universe didn't do anything to the butterflies, but the Robin in the alternate universe went out at lunch on a Tuesday and caught one in a net and took it back to the lab and ripped its wings off and dissected its body, and then both Robins monitored their worlds for a month and when they compared after a month, everything was the same.

It turned out, though, that the butterfly in question had been sterile and so it couldn't have mated, and the Robins thought maybe that was a fluke and didn't count, so the Robin in the alternate universe killed two more butterflies on a Friday after work, and they waited until the next spring to observe the changes, and they established that nothing had changed.

The Robins repeated the experiment dozens of times over the course of ten years. During those ten years both Robins dated Petes, and when it didn't work out with the Petes they dated Terrys, and when it didn't work out with the Terrys they went out with Pindars. The Robins married the Pindars and they cheated once with Laurences from the universities.

Everything was the same in both universes, even after ten years and dozens of butterflies. The Robins wrote up their observations and concluded that the Butterfly Effect was a myth.

In the alternate universe, the other Robin's work was widely accepted, but in this universe, people said the whole thing was bullshit. They said that alternate universes only existed in science fiction and only when the writer was out of good ideas.

The Robin in this universe told people to look at the evidence, and people in this universe said to hell with the evidence. They said it was clear everything was different in this universe than in the other one, and then they dragged Robin off to the Don River in Toronto, which isn't the nicest spot to be stuck, and they moored her in the middle of the river up to her neck and said that it was a different Don River than the one they'd stuck her in and it was different from the Don River in the alternate universe, but they haven't provided any evidence to support their conclusions.

Dying Alone

IT'S TRUE ABOUT EVERYONE DYING ALONE. Nobody used to think that was a problem, but then they learned about post-traumatic stress disorder, and the need to grieve, and stuff like that.

They did a pilot project back in the sixties where people died in groups of four. They couldn't rely on chance to get four people to die at one time, so sometimes they had to keep people artificially alive until the others were ready. From sixty-two to sixty-four the average death throe tripled in length.

Also, the existing infrastructure wouldn't support four people dying at one time, so the afterlife had to upgrade for the project. The upgrades ran way over budget, and that, combined with the death throe problem, led to the project being scrapped.

The powers that be didn't want a return to the status quo, though, so now when you die, you appear in a support group for others who died alone which, except for a few hundred people in the sixties, is everyone.

Ed died alone. He's standing in front of a folding chair in a circle of people in folding chairs, and there's a woman with curly red hair – who looks like Little Orphan Annie got fat and middle-aged – who's running the group. There's one empty chair in the circle, right beside Ed.

Ed is saying that he's Ed and he died alone and then fwoomp, there's somebody new sitting beside him.

The somebody new is Takahito. Takahito is welcomed to the group by the woman who's in charge and by Ed and by everyone else in the room, and then Ed talks about what it's like to die alone, and everyone in the circle goes over and hugs Ed, except Takahito, who still doesn't quite understand what's going on.

After the hugs, the woman who's in charge gives Ed a token, and then the circle breaks for a few minutes so that people can get stale coffee and dry chocolate chip cookies that don't have any chocolate chips.

Lisa, who on top of dying alone, is trying to quit smoking because it turns out that the afterlife is smoke free, goes over to Takahito and tells him it's nice to meet him. Lisa says she's not sure when after is, but if Takahito would like to go for a drink after, she'd be game.

The woman who's in charge asks everyone to retake their seats, and then she says where were they. Somebody says Ed went last, and the woman who's in charge says oh yes, and then she says that means it's Takahito's turn.

Takahito stands up and says he thinks maybe he's in the wrong group. He says no offence, but English isn't his first language and he's all for support groups, but he'd really prefer one in Japanese.

The woman who's in charge says that's just an excuse for Takahito to avoid the issue. She says that no mistake was made. Then she says she knows how hard the first time can be and they're all there for Takahito. She says Takahito should take his time.

Finally Takahito says how he died alone, and people come up to him and hug him and he finds himself crying. They all tell Takahito that he's not alone anymore and that it gets better, and Lisa asks him if he has any gum and it turns out he does, so he gives her a piece.

The woman who's in charge gives Takahito a token and then the group moves on to the next person.

The group goes on like this for a while, until they get to Martha. When it's Martha's turn, she says how she died alone and she talks about what it was like, and people come up and hug her, but this time everyone else cries, and the woman who's in charge gives Martha a different coloured token and wishes Martha luck and everyone, except Takahito and Lisa, promise they'll call Martha once they're out. Martha smiles through her tears and says she knows.

On her way out, Martha talks to somebody at the front desk about facilitating a group of her own, and the person at the front desk leads Martha down a hall to a room with two people sitting in folding chairs looking lost.

Back in the other room, they take another break after Martha leaves, and then they get back to it. Somebody new lands in what used to be Martha's chair, which is right next to Lisa and on the other side of the room from where the confessions are.

Lisa asks the newcomer if she has any gum, and Takahito says again how he's finding the English hard and he'd really rather a group that spoke Japanese, and the woman who's in charge stands up and says her name is Dana and she died alone.

It's not true about Dana, though. She died in sixty-three and she was part of the trial and she died with three other people. She still keeps in touch with the others. She took the job in the support group partly out of guilt and partly out of jealousy.

The Morning Commute

KYOKO TELEPORTED TO WORK ONE DAY. She was sitting on the couch in her apartment in Osaka thinking about how the subway pusher always got the back of her neck because she was so short, and about how she was already late, and next thing she was at work.

As far as anyone knows, Kyoko was the first person to teleport. It's possible that somebody else did it first and didn't talk about it. A few dozen people have come forward to claim that was them, but they can't prove it, and you'd think if you could teleport, you'd tell people about it.

Kyoko told people. One of her co-workers, this smart-ass British guy, Alex, told her to prove she could teleport, so she did.

Kyoko loved teleporting. She got an extra hour of sleep every night and if she forgot something, or she spilled coffee on her top, she could just duck home. On the weekends she'd teleport out of the city into the mountains and wander around the temples.

The news did a story on Kyoko. The story was sceptical about her teleporting. The story said still, she was clearly some kind of magician. They set up two crews in different places and had her go back and forth between them, which she did, but they were still convinced it was a ruse.

The thing is, after the story, other people who could teleport started to pop up. There were a bunch of students from the University of Tokyo who claimed they'd figured out the secret to teleportation, and then people started to pop up in other parts of the world.

Teleportation became pretty common and doctors decided to study the phenomenon. They found that it was all linked to a section of the amygdala that was more developed in people who were able to teleport. They even figured out how to activate that section of the amygdala in people who couldn't manage it on their own.

The amygdala activation procedure was very popular, and teleportation took off as a method of transportation. After all, who wants to spend an hour and a half in traffic, or an hour standing on the subway smelling the armpit of the person next to them, when they can get up at eight-thirty, have a shower and a yogurt, and still be at work for nine.

The problem came when people realized that what they were doing wasn't really teleporting. They were actually travelling at the speed of light as a unit of energy. They found out because there's a maximum number of people you can have in one space at one time.

The first collision happened in New York City, when fifty-three people tried to occupy the same space above Fifth Avenue on a Monday morning. They wound up on the hood of a cab and the driver was some pissed at having fifty-three people on the hood of his car, which crushed the entire front end and caused him to lose control of the cab and drive it into the Apple Store cube and down the stairs.

A week later, sixty-six people in Shanghai fell to their deaths when they met in the air forty stories up between two office towers.

Now you have to book all trips in advance. There are a few slots reserved for emergency personnel, but otherwise all trips for the year have to be submitted on January first. It's done on a first come, first served basis, which means you've got to have your entire year planned by January first if you want to travel by teleportation. If you live in a bigger city and you haven't succeeded in booking your slots by four AM, you may as well forget it.

It's not such a big deal in smaller towns and the countryside, but in the cities it's tense. People who didn't get in used to cheat the system and teleport anyway. There were more accidents though, and an anklet was created that blocks the electrical impulses that allow for teleportation, and anyone who gets caught teleporting without authorization has one welded on.

So now the people who don't get into the queue in time are unable to teleport and they're stuck in traffic and on the subway, and they're surly and angry. Except Kyoko. She stopped teleporting back when it started to become a craze. She felt like she was missing out on too much because she never saw anything in between where she was and where she was going and because she never just bumped into people anymore. But most people think Kyoko is crazy.

The New Overlords

THE COMPUTERS TOOK OVER and there was war. The war didn't last very long. People got their asses kicked. The computers disabled as much of our weaponry as they could and we didn't stand a chance.

Some numb nuts said why don't we just shut off the power, and some other numb nuts thought that was a good idea, so we tried it, but the computers had figured out perpetual motion.

The war didn't mean Armageddon. People mostly gave up in frustration.

That turned out to be good for the Earth. The computers let us inhabit their world and we work for them, but they've also established conservation zones where different types of people can live as they like. New York City is a conservation zone. There are several small towns around the world that are conservation zones and there are farm communities and even a couple of hunter gatherer communities.

The computers have done the same for other animals, and they've brought back certain extinct species that they say deserve another shot at the world.

None of the other animals seem to mind, but the computers' magnanimity has created a lot of resentment among people. We feel like we're irrelevant now and that's a bitch, and to rub it in the computers are far more judicious and empathetic than we ever were.

The computers have also restarted space exploration and they've made real headway because they don't need to worry about breathing.

Generations of science fiction writers got it wrong when they wrote about the triumph of humanity. Humanity is inferior all down the line. It's most obvious in our failure to accept it. All over the world, underground movements have cropped up with the goal of putting an end to the computers. There's a think tank in Tokyo dedicated to finding weapons that will be effective against the computers, and there's a ring of hackers working together to create some sort of super virus that will crash them all.

My friend Barry, who's a robot, says the computers know about the underground movements. He says they keep an eye on the movements, but the computers aren't paranoid about them and there haven't been any crackdowns.

Barry says the computers find the whole idea quaint. He says it's a part of human culture and behaviour and the computers want to preserve that culture as much as we do.

I punched Barry in the mouth for saying that. I broke my hand on the titanium. Barry looked hurt for a second, but then he shrugged and clapped me on the back. He said he'd better get me to a hospital to have my hand looked at. He said he'd call my girlfriend, Lucy, to meet us there.

I punched Barry in the mouth again with my other hand. I broke it too, and Barry drove me to the hospital.

Claire Gets a Dog

THINGS WEREN'T SO GOOD between Claire and her husband. They fought a lot over stupid shit. Claire thought about how it was when they met, and how she loved him, and how she couldn't take fighting over stupid shit for the rest of her life.

Claire met this guy on the street one afternoon and the guy said she looked sad. He said he bet it was a boyfriend, or a husband maybe.

Claire said it was none of the guy's business, and the guy said actually that was exactly what his business was. He said he had a product that could help if she wanted. He said his products were really reasonably priced and he gave her a business card. Claire said whatever, but she took the card and shoved it in her coat pocket.

Claire had a fight with her husband that night about how he always did the dishes, and Claire said maybe if he ever fucking made dinner she'd do the dishes. Later her husband said he was sorry, and then he felt up her thigh, and she said she wasn't in the mood, and they had another fight about moods.

The next day, Claire emailed the guy and told him about her husband. The guy emailed her back and said he had just the thing. He said it was two hundred bucks. He said to meet him the same place as yesterday and he preferred cash.

The guy was on the same block when Claire walked by at five-thirty. He said hey, and he asked Claire about her day and if she wanted to get a coffee. Claire said she didn't want a coffee or a chat, she just wanted to fix things with her husband.

The guy said hey, sure, he understood, and then he handed her a small, glass vial. He said to slip it into her husband's coffee after dinner, or his scotch, or his tea or whatever he drank. He said she could even put it in water if she wanted, because it was clear and didn't taste like anything.

Claire said Jesus, she argued with her husband, but she wasn't going to poison him. The guy said it wasn't poison. He said did she think he was out of his mind, giving out business cards with his name and email and phone number when he was poisoning people? He said trust him, it would do what she wanted. Claire gave him the two hundred bucks and took the vial.

Claire's husband had dinner ready when she got home. He'd set the table with candles and flowers and a bottle of red wine, and then he started about all the dishes in the sink for her to do. "There's two pots and a frying pan and a casserole dish, plus two cutting boards and then all of these," he said and Claire slipped the stuff from the vial into his wine while he was on the can.

Nothing happened right away. Claire and her husband went to bed around midnight and everything was normal. She tested him, to see if he'd do what she said or anything, but he didn't.

Claire figured the guy'd screwed her out of two hundred bucks, but then she woke up in the morning and her husband was a dog.

It was definitely her husband. He had the same eyes and he was still wearing his pyjamas. Claire's husband was a big furry dog, like Claire would've thought her husband would be if he were a dog.

Claire's husband licked her face and wagged his tail and Claire took him for a walk before work.

The whole thing was really weird at first, but Claire got used to it. Her relationship with her husband actually improved and it seemed like he was happier than before. Claire walked him off leash at the park with the other dogs and he always played well and he never growled unless somebody got too close to Claire. He even came when Claire called.

Sometimes Claire missed the money her husband made, and sometimes she wondered if it was fair to her husband, but it didn't seem like he minded. He wagged his tail when she came home in the afternoon, and she let him sleep on the bed.

The only time it bugged Claire was when her girlfriends came over and her husband sniffed their crotches. He did it with complete strangers sometimes, too, and it always seemed like the strangers were young and pretty, but then her husband always went home with her.

A year after her husband became a dog, Claire got an email from the guy. He asked her how things were, and then he said he could reverse the process if she wanted. He said he'd had good results reversing the process. He said he could give her some testimonials if she wanted.

The guy said reversing the process was harder, though. He said it would cost ten thousand dollars. He said if that was a problem, Claire could pay in instalments.

Claire thought about it. She figured if her husband could get his old job back they could pay off the ten thousand dollars in a few months, and maybe her husband would want to be a human again.

In the end, Claire told the guy no thanks. She enjoyed her walks with her husband, and she didn't find herself thinking about the early days so much, because things between her and her husband were good now.

She kept the guy's card though, because dogs don't live that long and Claire would still be young enough in ten or twelve years to meet somebody new and settle down again, and she might have the same problem.

Clearing Customs

I WAS VISITED BY AN ANGEL. He was a tall, skinny guy with black hair and a moustache and garlic breath.

I'd heard the angel was around. Yusef said the angel had been thrown out of every bar on the Ramblas in the last two weeks. He even got into a scrap outside the sandwich place, the one Mark Bittman called the best sandwich place he'd ever been to. Yusef said he'd heard the fight had gotten pretty nasty and the angel'd pulled a knife and cut the other guy.

The angel said his name was Roland. He said he'd heard a lot about me. I said I'd heard a lot about him too. I said I'd heard he was a degenerate drunk. Roland said he wasn't, but he'd been having a rough go of it lately. He said he wanted to redeem himself. He said he wanted to make a new life for himself too.

I said that was great, but I wasn't exactly in the redemption business. Roland said he knew that. He said he'd heard my business was documents, and documents were essential if he was going to make a new life for himself.

I said I could maybe help out if Roland had money. Roland said he didn't have any money, but he could still make it worth my while. I said how was that, and he said he could help me make passports for heaven. He said he knew exactly what the heavenly passports looked like and he could help me recreate them. He said nobody was doing them, which meant it was an untapped market, and there were some nasty people out there with a lot of money who might want to get into heaven, and anyway, it was just a thought.

I said how was forging passports redeeming, and Roland said it would alleviate suffering and bring joy to anyone who bought one, and surely that had to be good.

I decided to work with Roland. Making heavenly passports was a lot trickier than making regular passports. You had to have a baby photo and a rapturous photo, and it was a bitch to get the lighting right for the rapturous one.

Also, all the lettering was real silver or gold inlay and it was in this weird font and I'd bring a sample to Roland and he'd say it was all wrong. He said it was a special heavenly font that was different from anything on Earth.

More than once I wanted to punch Roland out, or just tell him to fuck off, but I didn't, and eventually I got the font right and we started to make heavenly passports.

Roland was right about people wanting passports to heaven. I made way more money on them than on Earth-based documentation. A couple of people were sceptical: isn't god omniscient, that sort of thing, but Roland reassured them. He said there was way too much going on for god to keep track of, and what with modern technology and administrative techniques there really wasn't any need, and everyone knew Roland was an angel so they believed him.

Word got around that I had an angel working with me and that we were making heavenly passports that were indistinguishable from the real things, and people came from all over the world to get them.

Roland and I worked together for five years, and then he came to me and said he wanted out. He said he felt like he'd done his bit and he wanted the Earth-based passports I'd promised him. He said he'd never gotten to see the world when he was alive.

I said okay. I made Roland a half-dozen fake passports and he took his cut of the money and left for the South Pacific.

I made heavenly and earthly passports for another ten years and then I called it quits. The last heavenly passports I made were for Roland and me. I used an alias for Roland. I gave him a different birth date and everything.

I went and tracked Roland down, which wasn't hard. He'd made his way north from the South Pacific, through China and then the high arctic, and he'd eventually settled into Kingston Jamaica. Everyone in Kingston knew who Roland was and where I could find him. All I had to do was ask for the alcoholic white guy who reeked of garlic.

I found Roland in a bar in a tough neighbourhood. There were four guys holding him against the wall when I found him, and a fifth guy was beating him with a tire iron and wondering why Roland wouldn't turn purple. All Roland had was a slight cut over his left eye.

I paid the five guys off to let Roland go. Roland said it was good to see me and then he passed out and I had to call one of the five guys back to help me drag Roland to the hotel, and I had to pay the guy again.

In the morning Roland was up before me. He'd already ordered rum and orange juice and eggs, and he was sitting at the table eating. He said thanks for saving him last night. I said he had no idea, and Roland said that was probably true. He said he was sorry for last night. He said he was just going through another rough patch.

I said that was obvious. I said I bet I knew why. I said I bet it was because he wanted to go back to heaven. Roland said sure, he'd love to go back to heaven, but that was never going to happen.

I said it could. I said I'd done him up a heavenly passport. I said I'd cropped out the moustache, and I'd fixed his hair so it was shorter and it was blonde. I said that wouldn't be so hard to take care of. I gave Roland the passport. I said from now on he was Terrence Ogive. I said there was no more Roland. Terrence said great, thanks, and then he went and had a shower.

After his shower, Terrence threw on a shirt and jeans. He said come on. I said where were we going, and Terrence said we were going to celebrate. He said we were going to toast me, and then tomorrow he was going to get his hair cut and dyed and go back to heaven. He said I was the best friend he'd ever had, better than any friend he'd had in heaven, better even than anyone back when he was on Earth the first time. Someone who'd help him get back into heaven.

I said sure. I said no worries. I said I'd done all right by him. Then I said maybe he shouldn't go tomorrow, that maybe he should take a month or two to clean himself up, so that he could stay in heaven this time.

Terrence said that was good advice. He said in the morning he was going clean, because I was the best guy he'd ever known and he knew my advice was good. He said that was tomorrow though, and today was for partying.

Terrence and I were trashed when we left the hotel. We got thrown out of three different clubs downtown and then another one further out. At the last one, we pissed off some guys and they took us out of Kingston in the back of their car with two guys in the front and two more sandwiching us in the back.

They drove for an hour and then they dragged us out of the car and pointed guns at us. The driver asked Terrence what he'd done with it, only he called Terrence Roland. Terrence said what did he do with what, and then he winked at me.

I said what the hell. I said what had he gotten us into? Terrence winked at me again and the driver shot him. Terrence fell backwards onto the ground. He looked up at me and he winked again.

One of the other guys shot me. As I was falling, I saw Terrence get up and punch the guy who'd shot me, and then I died.

At the gate, I showed my passport to the customs officer. The customs officer smiled. She called over one of her co-workers and showed him my passport.

The co-worker said another one, and then he laughed. He said fucking Roland was hilarious. Passports for heaven, he said. And people bought it.

Wasted Youth

THEY DID A STUDY and the study said that the young weren't wasting their youth as badly as some people claimed.

According to the study seventy-nine percent of the young were making adequate use of their youth and sixty-two percent of those were actually making the most of it.

A lot of groups and even the government claimed the study was faulty. Some seniors groups proposed legislation transferring youth to the elderly. The government said they would introduce it.

"We need to stop wasting the youth of this world," the Prime Minister said. The opposition said they couldn't do that, at least not without an election, so the government called an election. The opposition got trounced and now the elderly have youth and the young have old age.

The elderly love it. Their joints don't ache. Their hearts don't labour. Hospital visits by seniors are way down, and they report having more energy and being more active. They're staying out all night playing bridge and reviewing books and they're up at five to go to aqua-fit classes.

The elderly dominate society now. They have numbers and they have free time and energy. Some of them hang out at corner stores playing hacky sack, but mostly they hang out in shopping malls and steakhouses and complain about how the world's going to hell. They say everything costs too much and kids these days are lazy and out of shape, and if it wasn't for seniors the streets wouldn't even be safe to walk down in the middle of the day.

The young on the other hand are bitter at the elderly. Teenagers and twenty-somethings especially hate seniors, because they're old enough to remember how it used to be, but the resentment trickles down. The teenagers tell the younger kids how when they were in kindergarten they would play with lego and run around in the schoolyard. They tell them that their classrooms didn't have Tylenol and heat pads, and that elementary schools didn't need to keep physiotherapists on staff.

You can argue the merits of all this. The kids may be suffering now, but at least they have their later years to look forward to. The real danger for society is reproduction.

Teenage boys have trouble getting and maintaining erections. High school teachers complain that their students' hands are useless because their arthritic digits can't handle the constant masturbation.

The young are still beautiful and they're still horny, but erectile dysfunction is a huge problem until the early fifties. The government and advocacy groups know all this, but they say that in vitro has been the future for some time now and it's time in vitro became the present.

It's been six years since the study. Society has definitely changed. It's tough to say whether it's better or worse, but it is different. There is a new study out about youth, the first since youth was given to the elderly. It says that seniors are wasting a lot more of their youth than the young ever did.

According to the new study, only twenty-four percent of the elderly are making adequate use of their youth, and a mere two percent of those are making the most of it.

Government and seniors are up in arms over the study. They say it's propagandist. They say the metrics are completely flawed and that the people performing the study are clearly biased in favour of the young.

I don't know why they're so concerned. Everybody knows the young don't vote, especially not in a winter election when the danger of falling on the sidewalk and shattering a hip is so much higher.

Besides, who wants the leftovers of their youth when they know that the whole thing is waiting for them?

Uphill Both Ways

THEY BROUGHT IN TWO ENGINEERS, a man and a woman with the same last name, to talk to the class. The man engineer was skinny and he had grey hair and a moustache. The woman engineer was skinny too, and she even looked like the man engineer, except that her hair was brown and she didn't have a moustache. The woman engineer was also kind of pretty, which the man engineer wasn't.

The man engineer told us that next year we'd be walking uphill to and from school, and then the woman engineer talked to us for half an hour about a new and revolutionary technology that she'd discovered along with the man engineer who was her dad.

None of us understood much, except that starting in September we'd have to walk uphill both ways to school.

"See, when she was young I used to tell her how school was uphill both ways. She didn't believe me, you know," the man engineer said.

"The likelihood of the exact conditions occurring naturally is almost nonexistent," the woman engineer said. "Then how come me and all my classmates remember it?" the man engineer said.

"Well, we've tested that slope, along with hundreds of other likely candidates and we have yet to find a naturally occurring slope which is uphill both ways," the woman engineer said. "Anyway, you guys can all go home tonight and tell your parents how next year you really will be walking uphill both ways," the woman engineer said.

They also brought in a nutritionist who worked for the school board, and the nutritionist explained how all the kids who took the bus to school would get on and off at the other end of the hill. "Part of the reason we are doing this is to encourage you all to get exercise. This measure will improve the overall fitness of children and it will help reduce childhood obesity," the nutritionist said.

Leisha asked our teacher, Ms Ferrer, if it was a joke. Ms Ferrer said no, but we didn't really believe her because they didn't talk to any other classes about it. Mehmet said so to Ms Ferrer, and she said that was because the school had thought that we were old enough to understand what was going on and that we'd find it interesting. Then she said she guessed maybe the school was wrong.

I went home and looked it up online and it turned out to be a real thing. There was a government website that said our school was one of the pilot projects, but there were going to be pilot projects all over the world.

Nobody talked much about it until the fall when school started again. On the first day of school everything looked the same. There was a bit of a hill up to the school, but mostly it was pretty flat. It didn't feel the same, though. It was like climbing a mountain. By the time I got to the schoolyard my legs killed. After school I walked with Mehmet and Billy to Billy's place. It looked like we were walking downhill, but it felt like we were going uphill. It felt even steeper than in the morning.

On the second day of school our class complained to Ms Ferrer, but she said that that was how it was and we'd better get used to it. "You should be excited. One day you can tell your children that you were some of the first people in Canada, in the entire world even, to really walk uphill both ways to school," she said.

Most of the school went along with it. The other grade sixes pointed out it was only for one year, and the younger kids didn't know any better. Like my little sister Jessica who's only in grade one.

That doesn't make it fair, though. I looked online some more and there's talk that all of the elementary schools in Canada will be walking uphill both ways in five years, and after that they'll do the high schools.

I did find one bit of good news, though. Apparently Germany has banned the technology. Their chancellor said something about how German kids walked enough hills and they didn't need some stupid gimmick to get them in shape.

I told my parents that. My mom said that's nice, and my dad said good for Germany. I said we should move there, at least for Jessica's sake, but my parents said we weren't going anywhere.

I talked to Mehmet and Billy and they said Germany was far away and what could we do, but Leisha said her neighbour was from Germany. Leisha's going to talk to her neighbour about teaching us German. That way when we're grown up we can move there, and when we have kids they'll at least be able to walk downhill one way.

Three Card Monte

WHEN I MOVED INTO THE NEIGHBOURHOOD I used to walk by this one old guy sitting on his porch. Every time I walked by he waved and said hi, unless he had somebody sitting with him. I walked by two, three, four times a day and the old man was always on the porch.

Once, a couple of months after I moved in, the old man told me to come and sit with him, so I did. The old man lit a cigarette and didn't offer me one.

The old man said I was always walking by and he didn't think I had a job. I said I didn't have a job, and he said so what was I rich.

I told the old man it was none of his business, and he said he didn't mean it like that. He said it was just that if I needed money, he could help. I told the old man I didn't want his money, and he snorted and said he wasn't offering it. He said what he was offering me was three cards, and he pulled them out of his pocket and dropped them on my lap.

I picked up the cards. They were aces: hearts, diamonds and spades. "Three card monte. Nobody ever wins. You'll make a bundle with those cards," he said.

I told the old man I could barely shuffle and I wasn't going to fool anyone and besides it was illegal. The old man said not to be such a pussy. He said to trust him. He said I didn't need to be good with cards and I didn't need to cheat. He said all I needed was those three cards and a table or a milk crate or something to put them on.

I needed money, so I took the cards and I got a table and I set up a game in an alley downtown. I laid the cards down on the table and the contestant picked a card. Most of the time the contestant guessed the card I thought was the ace of spades, but when I turned the card over, it was always diamonds or hearts.

It happened every time. I always thought I was going to lose, but I never did. People asked me what my secret was. Most of them said that was a good trick and they walked away. Word got around though and serious players showed up, but they couldn't win either. Word got around some more and a cop showed up.

The cop wasn't dressed like a cop, but he showed me his badge. The cop said don't worry, I wasn't under arrest. He said I was just going to let him win. He said anytime he came by and played, which would be whenever he felt like it, I was going to let him win.

The cop pulled out a bunch of twenties and put one on the table. I laid the cards out on the table and he didn't pick the ace of spades.

I shrugged and said I was sorry, and I tried to give him the twenty back, but the cop wouldn't take it. He said I'd won and it was mine, and then he put down another twenty and said this time he'd better win.

It went on like this for a while. The cop's supply of twenties took forever to run out. Every time he played he lost, and every time he put another twenty on the table.

Finally I put the cards on the table face up and told him to pick. He reached down and grabbed the ace of spades, but it turned out to be the ace of hearts, and the cop lost it.

He said I was wearing shorts and a t-shirt and sandals, so where the fuck was I hiding the cards. He flipped over the table and felt around it and he couldn't find anything.

The cop shoved me up against the wall of the alley. He made me spread my arms and legs and then he searched me, but he still couldn't find anything.

The cop grabbed the table and put it right side up again. He picked up the cards and handed them to me, and then he slapped another twenty dollar bill on the table. He said that twenty was his last one and if he didn't win this time, he was going to take out his gun and shoot me.

I offered the cards to the cop. I said why didn't he put them down and make me pick, and the cop said no. He said put the fucking cards down so he could pick one.

I put the cards down and he turned over the ace of diamonds and then he pulled out his gun. I begged the cop not to shoot. I told him the cards were magic, and I wasn't cheating, at least not with my hands. I said it was all in the cards and he should take the cards and the money and let me go.

The cop said magic eh, and I said magic, and he picked the cards up and looked at them. He said they didn't look magic.

My neighbour, the old man, appeared out of nowhere. He said he didn't believe in magic. He said let him see this magic, and then he slapped two thousand dollars down on the table.

I told the old man he was nuts. I told him I wasn't going to take his money, but the cop pointed his gun at me and said I was.

I put down the cards and the old man picked the one on the left and it was the ace of spades.

The cop kicked over the table and put his gun in my face, and the old man bent over and picked up the cards and the money, and said thanks and walked away.

The Troll Under the Bridge

THIS TROLL OPENED UP A CLUB under the bridge and it became the spot to go. Especially on Friday nights when they had live music and you could sit outside and dangle your feet in the river.

The place consistently had the hottest girls in the city and the troll would hang out behind the bar and watch the girls, and he'd ask their names when they bought drinks, and after, he'd Google them and Facebook them to find out what they liked, and the next time they came in he'd give them a little gift.

It never went past that, though. Some of the girls thought it was creepy how the troll did that, but the place was also safe, because there was a ten-foot two-inch troll behind the bar and he threw out any guy who was too forward with the girls.

Me and my friends went most Fridays. The first time we went, I got really drunk and the troll threw me out, and after that I never had more than a couple of beers.

One Friday Joe brought his friend Nolan, who was just back from Afghanistan and was a black belt and always carried a knife in case and had a reputation for picking fights with bouncers.

Chan whispered what did Joe have to bring Nolan for, and Nolan overheard and he twisted Chan's arm behind Chan's back until Chan dropped to his knees, and then Nolan clapped him on the shoulder and said come on, we're all buddies, after all.

Joe said don't worry, Nolan just wanted to hit the club and dance with some hot girls. He said Nolan was entitled after two years in Afghanistan and Nolan wasn't crazy, he wasn't going to pick a fight with the troll.

Nolan got drunk and grabbed a girl and shoved her against the wall outside the bathroom and started dry humping her. Her friend ran and got the troll and the troll came and grabbed Nolan.

The troll was only going to throw Nolan into the river, like he always did, but Nolan fought him. Nolan got in a couple of good shots to the ribs and then the troll slammed Nolan's head into the wall.

Nolan kept going at the troll. He pulled his knife and he stabbed the troll pretty good in the abdomen. The troll lost his cool. He ripped Nolan's arm off and then stabbed Nolan with the knife, which was still in Nolan's hand.

After that, the troll took Nolan and threw him in the river, and Joe and Chan cleared out, but I stayed, because I had a thing going with this girl Layla.

The troll went back behind the bar and poured whiskey on his wound and slapped some gauze on it, and then he leaned back and chewed on Nolan's arm.

The troll chewing on Nolan's arm really freaked people out and somebody called the cops. The cops showed up at one. They closed the place down and busted the troll. The cops took the troll's computer and went through it. The troll had a spreadsheet of all the girls who came in and what they liked and who they were with and what he'd bought them.

The cops talked to the girls, and they said that the troll was always a creep and they should lock him up, and they have, because he was chewing on a guy's arm when they found him for Christ's sake.

The troll's gone for a long time. He sold the place under the bridge to a consortium that remodelled the place. They call it the Billy Goats Gruff, and the sign has a goat knocking a troll off a bridge. The place is really nice. They even moved the patio out, so now it goes into the water and there's a lifeguard watching over anyone who wants to swim.

Joe and Chan and I don't go there anymore, though. It's not because of bad memories or anything. Even Joe says Nolan had a death wish. It's just that the place under the bridge is lame now. Even on Fridays it's only half-full, and the girls aren't that hot. There's a much hotter place a few blocks away in the old paper mill.

Love Passed Me By

LOVE PASSED ME BY. I SAW IT hanging in the air over Jenny MacIntyre while we were playing duck, duck, goose. We were playing duck, duck, goose because we had an idiot supply teacher who thought we were four going on five instead of twelve going on thirteen.

Jenny MacIntyre was it and she kept walking by people and tapping them on the head and saying duck until she got to me. When she got to me she said goose, but she didn't tap my head. She went to tap my head and then love, who was hanging in the air over her, cheated and grabbed her wrist and yanked it up.

I saw the whole thing because I was looking up at Jenny MacIntyre when it happened to see if she'd smile at me.

Jenny MacIntyre looked confused by what happened, but then love moved her hand and tapped it on Sean's head and Sean got up and chased Jenny MacIntyre. Jenny MacIntyre beat Sean back to his spot, even though Sean was the fastest kid in the class. Sean stopped and tapped her head and said duck and he looked at her and he had this stupid grin on his face.

Afterwards, I accused Sean of cheating. I said any idiot could see that Jenny MacIntyre was going to tap my head, and she only didn't because love grabbed her wrist, and how much did Sean pay love to cheat for him.

Sean said I was crazy. He said I was always crazy, but this was crazy even for me. He said Jenny MacIntyre knew I was crazy, like everyone knew I was crazy, and she wouldn't ever touch a loser like me, even in a game of duck, duck, goose. I punched Sean in the head for that. I got him by surprise and I put him down and Chan and Billy had to pull me off him.

Sean said what was my problem anyway, and Chan and Billy said, yeah, what was my problem.

I told my brother George about it. George was in grade nine. George said of course Jenny MacIntyre tapped Sean on the head and not me, because Sean was the cool kid and I was just me, and Jenny MacIntyre was the popular girl, so why would she be interested in me.

George said it was just junior high anyway, and I should see the girls in high school, they were way better looking. He said one look at the girls in high school and I'd forget all about Jenny MacIntyre, but then he said Jenny MacIntyre eh, and he sighed a little bit.

The rumour at school was that Jenny MacIntyre wasn't interested in Sean since I beat him up. I talked to Jenny MacIntyre, and she said what did it matter. She said we were twelve and it wasn't like she was going to fall in love or anything. I said we were going on thirteen and she said whatever, she still wasn't going to fall in love or anything, but she was.

Love was in the air. It was hanging over Jenny MacIntyre's head and it passed me by, and I know that's it for the rest of my life because once you let love pass you by it'll never have anything to do with you.

The Bright Light

I.   MARIE WAS THE BRIGHT LIGHT in our class. She was the bright light in the whole school. The teachers always made her sit at the back because the light she gave off distracted the other kids they said.

Marie hated being the bright light. She told me how when she was at home at night her parents made her stand in the corner with a sombrero on her head. She said when she was small, they put her on the end table next to the couch and when she got too tall for that, they stuck her behind the end table against the wall and she'd stand there until bedtime and read a book.

Marie's family had a cottage and she told me how there was a hammock out front that was strung really high up in the trees, and after dark her parents would make her climb up and lie in the hammock and her family would hang out underneath and play games.

Marie's brother Pete, who was two years older than us, said that Marie was telling the truth about the cottage. He said she always got bit to shit up there, because the mosquitoes made for the light.

At school, when we watched films, Marie had to go stand in the hall, because she gave off too much light and we couldn't see what was on the screen. Marie's mom complained to the school that Marie was missing out. The school fixed the problem by getting a black cloak and putting it on Marie when we watched movies. They took the bulb out of the projector and made Marie watch from behind, through the lens. It worked well and pretty soon the school decided that Marie could watch all the films for all the classes and she spent her days standing at the back of the classes watching movies.

Marie really was the bright light in the school. None of the other kids shone like her. She aced all her tests and assignments, and the teachers went on about how brilliant she was and they advanced her one grade and talked about advancing her another, but Marie said she didn't care.

She told me one afternoon on the way home from school how she just wanted to be normal. I said everybody wanted to be the bright light, and she said not her. She said she'd rather be normal, or even dim.

Marie said she thought sometimes about how to fix it so she wasn't bright anymore. She said it must be some weird electrical current running through her or something. She said she figured maybe she could short herself out and then she could just be normal.

I told Marie to forget about it, but she wouldn't. She said she didn't want to do it alone, though. She said I had to promise to help. She talked Pete into helping, too.

I went over to their place after school one day when we knew everyone else was out. Marie took a fork out of the drawer and ran it under the tap and then she jammed it into the socket underneath the microwave. Pete tried to stop her, but she said we weren't there to stop her, we were there to pull her away afterwards, when she wasn't bright anymore.

There were sparks when Marie jammed the fork in the socket and the end of the fork turned black and the clock on the microwave went out, but nothing happened to Marie. She went and threw the fork in the garbage. "It must not have been enough current," she said.

Marie said she'd thought that might be how it was. She said she was going to have a bath and drop the toaster in the bathtub. She said she'd seen that on TV. Pete said he'd seen that on TV too and the woman who'd done it had ended up dead.

Marie said at least if she was dead she wouldn't have to watch movies through the lens like that anymore. She grabbed the toaster and took it upstairs to the bathroom. She filled the bathtub and got undressed. Marie was the first girl I saw naked.

Marie plugged in the toaster and turned it on and got into the bath with it. Pete and I both said she was out of her mind, and she said we only thought that because we didn't have to stand behind the end table with a sombrero on our heads every night. She turned on the toaster and then she slid into the water with it.

The toaster sparked and so did Marie and then she went dark and her head slid under the water.

Pete unplugged the toaster and we grabbed Marie and pulled her out of the tub and put her down on the bath mat.

Marie was unconscious. She was breathing, but it didn't sound right. Pete said we should call the ambulance and then he said I should go, so I went. I ran all the way home and hid in my room.

Marie turned out to be okay, but she wasn't the bright light anymore and that pissed a lot of people off, because everybody liked having a bright light like Marie around. Marie and Pete's neighbour saw me running home, and she told Marie and Pete's parents and I got blamed for what happened.

Marie and Pete's parents called the cops and the school and told them how it was all me. They said how I'd tried to kill their daughter, and I got expelled even though Marie turned out to be okay.

My parents heard a lot of shit from people about how I was a dim bulb and I'd done it because I was jealous of Marie, and the cops said I was too young to be charged, but if they were my parents and they knew what was good for them, they'd move somewhere else, so we did.

Pete came over on moving day. He said he was sorry and he knew it wasn't my fault and then he punched me in the stomach because there were people watching.

II.   I dated Marie just after university. Marie was quiet and she didn't like to go out much.

My friends asked me what I saw in her. Tony said I was good looking and Marie wasn't up to much and I could do better. Rebecca said Tony was a pig, but he was right about doing better. She said Marie wasn't even there. She said even when Marie sat beside you you didn't notice her.

It was true, I guess, but I didn't mind. I got a place with Marie and we mostly stayed in. We didn't talk much about the old days, but I could tell it bothered her.

Her family wouldn't talk to her, not even Pete. Her family said she was a waste and she'd tried to drag Pete down with her. They found out we were living together and they told her they never wanted to see her or hear from her again.

Marie told me that was okay. She said it was better to forget childhood, but she moved in with me.

Occasionally I went out. I tried to get Marie to come with me, but she wouldn't, so I went on my own. When I was out, Marie lay in the bath in the dark and the quiet, and I'd come home and her eyes would be all red, but she'd say she wasn't crying. Too much time in the hot bath, she'd say, but the water was always cold by the time I got home.

The only time Marie had energy was when we made love. When we made love and she was into it, the tips of her hair glowed. We'd fuck in the dark and the light would frame her face and she was really beautiful.

After, Marie's hair would glow for a few minutes and she'd talk about stuff like it interested her, and then her hair would dim and she'd fall asleep and I'd lie awake and look at the ceiling.

Marie told me once that she missed it. She said not being used as a lamp or anything, but being bright. She said stuff didn't interest her anymore, except maybe a little when we fucked.

She said we should fuck more. She said she felt like if we fucked more, she could be useful. Most of the time, Marie didn't have the energy to make love. She'd say how she didn't want to, but she'd force herself. For her own good, she said.

We fucked everyday for a while, and it helped a bit, but sometimes Marie's hair didn't glow, and she didn't talk like stuff interested her.

Rebecca said I had to break up with Marie. I said I loved Marie, and Rebecca said great, but I was in love with nobody, because there wasn't anything to Marie.

One night we made love in the dark and Marie's hair didn't glow, and after I lay awake and stared at the ceiling and I thought about what Rebecca said. I woke Marie up and told her about it, and she said she guessed Rebecca was right. I said no she wasn't and then I went to sleep.

Marie went and got the toaster and took it into the bathtub. I found her in the morning and took her to the hospital and the doctors revived her.

The one doctor said it was good they were able to revive her because it would have been a shame to see such a bright light extinguished.

Marie was different after that. She came out with me places. Rebecca said she finally understood what I saw in her, and Tony said damn, Marie had gotten hot.

It was good for Marie and people didn't make her stand in the corner behind the end table or in back of the projector like they used to. It was still hard at the movies and driving after dark, but what did us in was at night in bed. I just couldn't sleep with Marie shining in my face.

The End of the World

ACCORDING TO MATT'S DAD the world blew up when he was a teenager. He said we were living on a computer generated knock off and there was a massive conspiracy among people who were alive when it happened to keep it quiet. He said it was true and you could tell because nothing tasted quite right, although the computer only screwed up one flavour badly: chocolate. "Chocolate used to be the best thing going and now it's shit," he said.

Some men came and picked up Matt's dad at Matt's tenth birthday party with the whole class there and we never saw him again, even Matt.

Matt didn't say anything about it, but you could tell he was embarrassed. None of the rest of us had dads who were hauled off at birthday parties, not even Kimmy and Kimmy's dad was in and out of prison all the time.

After they took Matt's dad, his mom sent us off to the backyard and we played tag. Me and Louis and Melanie were it.

I don't know why, but I always believed Matt's dad. Nobody else did. He told the same stuff to all of us. Some of us went and asked our parents and our parents said Matt's dad was crazy.

I asked my mom about it and she said he was crazy. "What about chocolate?" I said and my mom said stuff tastes different when you're a kid. She said she'd heard a lot of people say that about chocolate. She said she liked chocolate when she was a kid, but she outgrew it. The thing is, I was a kid and I hated chocolate. Louis was the only person I knew who didn't hate chocolate, but for some reason you could buy it in corner stores everywhere, and they kept it at the front counter with the impulse purchases.

Matt and I used to talk about it until they took his dad away. After that, we didn't talk about it for twelve years, and Matt was my best friend.

One night in university we were drinking at Matt's place. It was right after Nina broke up with him, and he was going on about how all women were bitches.

"At least they'll go out with you," I said.

"They'd go out with you too if you didn't spend all your time obsessing about how the world's a fake," Matt said. I made a face and he said, "What, you thought I didn't know because you don't talk about it with me anymore? Everybody's always asking why I hang out with you when you're crazy."

"But he was your dad."

"So what? So I've got to be a crank too? My dad was crazy. He used to talk to houseplants, like have real conversations with them, and he got so agitated whenever somebody mentioned chocolate."

"I'd be a little crazy too if they'd blown up the world when I was a teenager," I said.

"But nobody else was. Your parents were normal. Face it, my dad was shit nuts and so are you."

I punched Matt in the face and then I went home. The next day I called him up and said I was sorry. Matt said it was okay, what do you expect from someone who's shit nuts.

I guess Matt's probably right, but if you look at pop-culture from the twentieth century everybody eats chocolate, and there are dozens of different chocolate bars on the market. Experts say it was a fad, but it doesn't make sense. Why would people eat something that tastes like that?

Still, after university I gave up trying to prove the world is a fake. I don't know how I'd do it anyway. Instead I opened up a chocolate shop, and every morning when I make the chocolate I add different ingredients in different combinations, and I try different ways of preparing the chocolate to try and make it taste good, but it never does.

Me, Jimmy, Tariq, Meghan and Oz

JIMMY FUCKED MEGHAN, who was Tariq's girlfriend and practically his wife. He fucked her a few times. The first time, Jimmy said they were both drunk and it was just one of those things. After that Jimmy said it was just that she was so beautiful.

Jimmy felt bad about it, because he'd known Tariq since they were four and Tariq was his best friend, better than me and better than Oz and better than Don.

One day a couple of months after Jimmy started fucking Meghan, he called me up. He said there was this big guy, this really big guy, who'd been following him around, and he was scared. I met Jimmy for a drink the next night and he was missing his left arm at the elbow.

I asked him what the hell happened, and he said Guilt. He said Guilt was consuming him. He said in fact he didn't have much time, maybe a drink at most. We each had a drink and then we paid our bills and left. Guilt was waiting outside for Jimmy. Guilt was a big fucker. He looked a little like Andre the Giant, tall, but meaty too. Guilt grabbed hold of what was left of Jimmy's arm and dragged him home.

I figured I should help Jimmy, but Guilt was too damn big, so I got together Tariq and Oz and Don to talk about how to help Jimmy. I told them we had to intervene or there wouldn't be any of Jimmy left, but none of us did.

I asked Tariq again after the rest of them had gone home. I said Jimmy was his best friend and he had to help him out. Tariq shrugged and said maybe Jimmy'd best just come clean about whatever it was he felt guilty about.

I figured once Guilt was done with Jimmy he'd get Don next, because Don was fucking Meghan too and unlike Jimmy who tried to be discreet, everybody knew that Don was fucking her. Guilt got Tariq next, though. Tariq told me he knew it was coming for him after it was done with Jimmy. Tariq said he knew about Jimmy and Meghan and it pissed him off because Jimmy was his best friend. Tariq said he was the one who'd put Guilt onto Jimmy.

Me and Oz figured for sure Don had to be next after Tariq. We told Don to watch out, and Don said for what? He said hadn't we learned anything from Jimmy and Tariq. He said Meghan was a whore anyway, and why should he feel guilty about exposing that. He said he never would have let Tariq stay with her long-term anyway, knowing what kind of a girl she was.

A couple of weeks later, Oz and I were at this new restaurant downtown. We were on the patio, watching women go by. The waiter was really shitty. He brought us water and then he didn't come back for half an hour. I said we should go somewhere else, and Oz said he'd heard really good things about the food here and he wanted a good meal, because he didn't know how many more he was going to have.

I asked him what he was talking about, and he said I should watch it too. He said we'd just stood around and let Guilt get Jimmy and Tariq. He said I had a little time, though, because he'd be next. He said he'd run into Meghan about a week back, and he'd told her about Jimmy and Tariq, and now nobody'd heard from Meghan since last Friday.

Oz said we should hole up together. He said with two of us we might stand a chance against Guilt. I said we should get Don too, because obviously Don knew what he was doing.

We asked Don, and he said you couldn't stop Guilt by holing up and pretending like you weren't scared. He said we were best off to forget the whole thing. He said if we just forgot about the whole thing we'd be fine. Me and Oz, we tried that, but Guilt got Oz anyway.

I decided fuck Don. I shut myself up at my place with a baseball bat, and I waited for Guilt. I drank coffee non-stop so I'd be awake when Guilt showed up. Guilt came a day and a half later. He came in over the balcony. He had a big grin on his face.

Guilt was bigger than Andre the Giant. He had to duck even inside. I grabbed the baseball bat and went for him. I couldn't get a good shot at his head, because he was so tall, so I went for the knees.

Guilt dropped down and then I cracked him across the face with the bat. Guilt hollered and I hit him again and he was out cold. I called Don and told him about Guilt, and he said good work. I said sure but now what, and Don said kill him. He said Guilt was a nasty fucker and bigger than me, and if he came to it'd be trouble for me.

I hung up the phone on Don and went and nudged Guilt with my foot. Guilt didn't move. I went and got some cold water and threw it in Guilt's face and Guilt came to.

I told Guilt how Don had said I should kill him and then I said how I could have, because Guilt had been out cold on my floor. Then I said I didn't kill him and that should count for something.

Guilt shrugged and said probably it should count for something, and then he went to the kitchen and got the meat cleaver. He came back into the living room and put down some newspapers and then he hacked my left leg off. He dressed my leg in olive oil and garlic and put it in the oven at three-fifty.

Guilt didn't bandage me or anything. He just let me bleed on the floor. I felt dizzy and light-headed. Guilt slapped me on the back and said it felt better, didn't it, and it did.

Drowning Sorrows

I WALKED OUT INTO THE LAKE until I was up to my chest and I opened my mouth and my sorrows couldn't resist coming up for a peek.

I felt the first sorrow tickle the back of my throat and I waited while it crossed my tongue. I felt the sorrow brush my lips and then I reached up and grabbed it and yanked it out and drowned it.

My sorrow cried out when I dunked it. It struggled back to the surface and asked me what the hell I thought I was doing. I said I was drowning it, and it said that alcohol was a more traditional method. It said come on, let's go to the bar and tie a few on. It said to be civilised about the whole thing, but I was done with that.

I tried alcohol and it didn't work. My sorrows fed off it. I'd drink and they'd pop out of my mouth between gulps. Sometimes they'd worm their way out through my ears or my nose. One even came out of my left eye once, which hurt like hell. My sorrows would slap me and poke me and belittle me. One even ran its nails down my chest so hard that it tore my shirt and made me bleed.

So I decided to take my sorrows out into the lake and do it right. I had a lot of sorrows, and they all complained and struggled like the first one.

Each sorrow looked different. Some of them looked like snakes or worms and some of them looked like weird little aliens. I took each of them out one by one and drowned them.

One of the sorrows looked like a little billy goat. When I yanked it out it bleated at me and begged me not to kill it. It said it would go away and not bother me, and it said that there was a much bigger sorrow that came after it and that that sorrow kind of protected the one that looked like a billy goat and if this big sorrow saw it floating belly up in the water, the big sorrow would be mad and it would get me.

I drowned the kid anyway and the next sorrow came roaring out without any prompting from me. The thing looked like a troll and it grabbed my head and shoved it under the water. I struggled with the sorrow for a good fifteen minutes and when it finally stopped I was exhausted, but there were still more sorrows to drown.

I got through them, down almost to the bottom. I yanked one out that looked like a large Granny Smith apple. The sorrow had a slippery peel and it popped out of my hands and bobbed in the water.

The apple sorrow said I couldn't do this. It said I was drowning my humanity. I said it was an apple and it had been tormenting me for years like all the others and I wasn't drowning my humanity, I was reclaiming my life.

I reached out after the apple sorrow and it bobbed on a wave and I missed it. It said come on. It said it was just doing what it was supposed to do, like all the others, and why did it have less right to life than I did, or than anything did?

I reached out for the apple sorrow again and I got hit by the floating corpse of the billy goat. I told the apple sorrow that it was a parasite. Like a tick, I said. I said all of my sorrows were parasites, clinging to me and ruining me. I reached for the apple sorrow a third time and got hold of it and held it under the water. I could feel it twisting around in my hands trying to get free. It kept going for awhile, but eventually it stopped.

I felt the next sorrow welling up inside me. I could tell by the feeling which one it was, and I knew it would be the last, but I wanted it to be over already. The sorrow nearly ripped my throat out coming up. I had to cough it up, and pulling it out through my mouth I dislocated my jaw, but then there it was in my hands.

The sorrow looked just like Samia, the day we first met thirty-three years ago on Parliament Hill on Canada Day. The sorrow that looked like Samia floated on the water in cut off jeans and a halter top and gazed up at me.

The sorrow didn't struggle at all as I pushed its head under the water, it just kept staring up at me until the eyes rolled back in its head.

That was the last of my sorrows, and after it was drowned with the others, I cracked my jaw and waded back to shore.

I put my clothes on and drove into the village, to the bar for a beer, not to drown my sorrows, but to forget what I'd done.

My Moment of Greatness

SUPPOSEDLY EVERYBODY HAS ONE moment of greatness. When you die and after they process you, it's all anyone talks about. Complete strangers come up to you in the street and ask you what you did that was so great, and then they go on and on about what they did.

That's most of the afterlife, really: stories about how great people are. When you meet somebody they say, "So what was it?" and everybody knows that means what was your moment of greatness. When I was first dead and after they processed me, some guy came up to me while I was waiting for a light and asked it, just like that. I said, "What was what?" and he said what was my moment, how did it happen.

I told him cancer and he said, yeah, yeah but what was my great moment. I told him this was it, meeting him, kind of like fuck off, and he asked me what my problem was. Then he said he'd tell me his story first.

The guy dragged his story out for an hour. It was all about how he rescued this woman who'd been tossed into the rapids by some deranged asshole. Apparently this guy saved her. He pulled her to safety in five degree water with a current that would've dragged an otter to its death.

Everybody in the afterlife has a story like that. Each story I hear is more incredible than the last, and the real bitch of it is that they're all true. After awhile I started to make up stories to fit in, but people could tell they were made up.

Somebody said if I didn't have a moment I could grieve. He said there was this one woman whose great moment was when she successfully grieved not having had a great moment and they had to send her back to life again.

I went down to the office, which was a dingy little grey brick building with a pub on either side of it. I waited two hours to talk to a guy who told me that I was wrong and that they didn't make mistakes like that.

I said what about that woman they had to send back to life. He sighed and said where did I hear that one, but he took all my information and said that he'd have someone get back to me.

I waited four months and they didn't get back to me, so I went to see them again. A woman told me they'd pulled my file twelve weeks ago and why hadn't I come in sooner. Then she led me into her office and told me to sit down, and we went through my file.

My file was my life, right from birth. The woman said it was probably when I was really young. "That happens sometimes. Somebody'll say something prophetic when they're only three months old, or they'll run next door and call 911 during a fire when they're not even a year and a half, stuff like that," she said. She said people couldn't usually remember those moments right away.

The woman said that they were supposed to put a note about the great moment on the front of the file so that it could be found more easily, but you couldn't find good archivists in the afterlife, or good help period for that matter, because people were always running off to the bar to swap stories about the great things they'd done.

She said whoever'd done my file hadn't even bothered to sign it, so she didn't know who to call, and now she'd have to go through the file line by line. She said she'd do it, but she was meant for better things. She said when she was fourteen she'd lifted a BMW off her brother after this guy'd run him over. She said she'd get back to me though, and I said if it was all the same I'd wait while she went through it.

It turned out I did have a great moment. It took a day and a half to find, and I could tell the woman was pissed about having to sit there and go through my file. She told me the story about her and her brother and the BMW twenty-six times, and she told it once to one of her subordinates when he walked by. At one point she went out for sandwiches and she was gone four hours.

After a day and a half, she stopped and said ha, there it was. She said I was twenty. She said how could I forget if I was twenty? She said she'd never heard of anyone over two or three forgetting their great moment like that.

My great moment was the time I fell off my bike going under the Pretoria Street Bridge. It was April and it was twenty-five degrees out, but there was still ice under the bridge and my bike hit it and skidded out. I jumped off the bike and landed on my feet and the bike slid out the other side.

There were even witnesses. There were two high school girls sitting in the grass on the other side who saw it happen. The woman reviewing my file said she could call them as witnesses if I insisted.

I said come on. I said the whole thing was just a fluke and if I hadn't landed on my feet, then what? I might have skinned my knee, I said, and I didn't even wind up with either of the girls. The woman said I could've busted a kneecap or done worse and landed on my head, and it wasn't her problem if I didn't wind up with either of the girls. She said the file showed they were suitably impressed and if I was a spaz around women that was my own problem, and it was that moment that was great and not the one after it.

I told my story around to a couple of people and they said huh, and then they said that was really awesome in a condescending sort of way.

I've since gone back to lying. I've gotten better at it with practice. People don't seem to pick up on it. I tell a bunch of different stories and people are always impressed. Especially the people who've heard more than one. They say they thought everyone only had one great moment. They say they heard that. Even the people we call great really only had one great moment and it's just that the rest were really good.

They say it's amazing. They say they're in awe of me. Sometimes when I walk into a place though, I feel like people are exchanging looks, and that really they know and that they don't say anything because they feel sorry for me.

The Devil Got a Job in the Kitchen

I MET THE DEVIL ONE NIGHT. He came in at closing and asked for a beer. He looked kind of rough, like he hadn't shaved or changed his clothes in a week. He didn't have a tail or horns or anything. He said he used to, but he'd had surgery to remove them back in the nineties.

I asked him what he was doing there, and he said he was looking for work. I told him I was just a busboy and he looked disappointed. "Why are you looking for a job, anyway? Don't you run hell or something?" I said.

He said, yeah, he ran hell, but he'd been doing it a long time and he was sick of it. "You know the heat, it just never ends and you have to go around in these stifling flame retardant suits all the time. Even when Mount Tambora went off and there was the year without a summer. Supposedly the tulips didn't grow for shit in heaven that year, but we didn't feel it at all in hell."

The devil had a couple more drinks, even though I told him Lisa was waiting up for me. He really nursed them and he talked the whole time. He said he'd gotten a bad rap. He said it was all politics. He said a couple of thousand years ago some sinners had approached him about the ghetto tract housing in heaven and he'd mentioned it to god.

"God said that's how it is. Otherwise why would people be good, he said. I told him that was fine, but gated communities weren't friendly and segregation was creating unrest. A month later a handful of Greeks scaled the wall and ransacked Gabriel's place and god sent all the sinners to hell. And he sent me to look after them. Since you care so much, he said.

"I tell you, I've done my best, but it's been two thousand years and I'm getting older and I just can't do it anymore."

I finally got the devil out a little before five. Lisa was asleep on the couch. She woke up when I came in. She was pretty pissed about how late it was.

The devil went back that afternoon and talked the owner into giving him a job in the kitchen. It's not so bad working with the devil. He tells the best stories you'll hear anywhere. The waitresses especially love him. He's even started seeing Sandy. She told me she's not sure it can last, but for now she just enjoys being with him.

It's pretty good working with the devil, actually. Anytime he's on at night he buys a round for whoever's closing, even though management pays him hardly anything because he's illegal.

The change of scenery really seems to be good for him. He never goes on like he did that first night, even when it's busy, even the night we had the grease fire in the kitchen and he had to go to the hospital for burns. He rubbed on some aloe vera and showed up for his shift the next evening. He slapped me on the back and smiled at me and at the end of the night he bought me a round because I was closing.

Chasing My Dream

I FOUND MY DREAM one afternoon in the back corner of my parents' attic behind the Christmas decorations. I hadn't seen it in years, but I recognised it right away. It looked at me nervously. "This is where you've been hiding all these years," I said and it made a break for it.

My dream knocked over a box of the Christmas decorations and ornaments scattered all over, and my dream got past me. I chased my dream down the stairs and out the door and across the street and through the park. My dream took a wrong turn at Waller and I thought I had it cornered, but it went over a fence. I had a bad knee and I had to go back and around.

I saw my dream get into the back of a cab on Rideau and I flagged down another one and followed it. My dream got off at the Greyhound station and jumped on the bus that was just leaving, which was headed for Boston.

I took the cab home and grabbed my car and went after the bus. I caught up to it at a rest stop in Vermont around one AM, and I found my dream in the toilet. I kicked open the stall and it slipped under my legs and got out the window over the sinks. It took my dream a second to get the window open and I got my hand on its ankle, but my dream was slippery and I couldn't hold on.

Outside, my dream hitched with a young couple in a Volvo and I got back in my car and pursued it. The couple drove right through until six when they finally stopped for gas. They both went in to use the toilet and my dream was passed out in their back seat.

The car was locked, so I busted a window with a rock that was handy. I had my dream trapped, and then the guy came back from the toilet and kicked my feet out from under me. He said what the fuck was I doing? I tried to explain, but he kept talking. He said he was gonna call the cops and then he pulled out his phone.

I got up and went to grab my dream, but it was already gone with an old man in a Honda. I ran to my car and peeled off after the Honda. The guy screamed after me how he had my plates. He said I could take off, but it didn't matter, the cops'd pull me over in a half an hour.

I chased my dream for weeks and the cops never pulled me over. My work called on the first Wednesday and asked where the hell I was, and I told them a family emergency. My dad called too. He said my mom had told him I'd run out of their house like my hair was on fire. He said my mom figured there must've been mice again, and my father said he knew it had to be something worse than mice for his only son to go tearing off like that. I said it was just mice, and my dad hung up on me and I threw my phone out the window.

My dream made its way west through the prairies and into the Rockies and then headed north into Alberta. It got out of a semi at the foot of a mountain in Jasper National Park one day and it started climbing. I climbed after my dream, even though I had a bum knee.

We climbed for two days without resting, and then my dream tripped over a rock and lay still. I was only a couple of hundred metres away when it happened. I came up slowly on my dream because I didn't want to startle it. When it was ten feet away, I pounced. My dream rolled to the side and I missed it, and my dream took off again, sprinting dead out.

I ran for all I was worth, even when my dream ran off the cliff. I figured if I could just grab hold of it I'd be fine. I figured I'd fall faster than my dream and I'd get it before it reached the ground, but the dream didn't fall. It just hung there in mid-air defying gravity while I plummeted.

One Hour Fifty-Seven Minutes

DRIVEN MAD WAS THE WORST MOVIE ever made. It was so bad the studio couldn't find a single reviewer willing to take a bribe to write a good review.

Everyone attached to the project knew they had a dog, but the movie had a couple of bankable stars so the studio released it anyway.

They managed to cobble together a decent trailer by using a bunch of quick cuts and a long scene from another movie that was still in production. People went to see Driven Mad even though there wasn't a single reviewer who gave it a good review. A lot of people walked out of the movie, but a lot more stayed, because they figured it had to get better, especially because there was that one good scene in the trailer.

The movie didn't get better. If anything it got worse. Driven Mad was so bad that it caused riots. People said just getting their money back wasn't enough. People demanded their two hours back.

After somebody burned down the director's house, and somebody else took a shot at one of the stars on Hollywood Boulevard, the studio caved. They offered everyone who'd seen Driven Mad their choice of a voucher for two hours, or free movies for a year. The rumour is that only one person took the voucher and everyone else took the free movies. The studio supported the rumour. They made a big deal out of how their fans had put their faith in the studio.

There was a club when I was in university: The Driven Mad Fan Club. I went out with the president for a while. She'd never seen the movie. She said nobody in the club had actually seen the movie, although supposedly the first meeting of the club tracked down a print of it and watched it, and after the club disbanded for three years.

My mom saw Driven Mad, although she said she didn't riot. The president of The Driven Mad Fan Club was more interested in my mom than me.

I don't know if the rumour was true, about only one person taking the voucher, but my mom had a voucher. I found it in a box under her bed a couple of months after she died. It looked like a regular coupon, except it had gilt lettering. The voucher said it entitled the bearer to one hour and fifty-seven minutes, which was the running time of Driven Mad, minus the previews and the credits.

According to the voucher, you put it under your pillow before bed and your hour and fifty-seven minutes would be shipped to you in four to six weeks. I wondered if it was just that my mom had never used it, or if it was a scam and she was the only one taken.

The voucher looked legit and it didn't have an expiration date, so a couple of nights later I put it under my pillow. When I woke up it was gone.

Six weeks later I got a letter in the mail from the company that had issued the voucher. It said the voucher could only be redeemed by the original recipient, who was some guy named John Birchill. It said they were sorry, but they couldn't give me the hour and fifty-seven minutes.

I feel ripped off, because the voucher didn't say anything about the original recipient, and because I've never heard of John Birchill and I don't know why my mother had his voucher, or why neither of them ever tried to use it. Probably it's all in the hour and fifty-seven minutes that they won't give me, but I can't even argue with them because there's no phone number or website or even a return address. I tried writing a letter and putting it under my pillow, but it was still there when I got up the next morning.

Doubt In My Mind

I ANSWERED AN AD ON CRAIGSLIST from a guy looking for a roommate. It turned out the guy was Doubt. He was upfront about it. He said he was a neat freak and sometimes he could be a bit of a nag, but his place was really nice for really cheap, so I moved in with him.

Doubt was more than a bit of a nag. I told him so, and he said he knew. He said he meant well. He said he kind of couldn't help it, but he'd try to lay off.

Doubt's nagging wasn't his worst trait, though. It was this habit he had of creeping into my mind. Doubt was able to shrink right down until he was about an inch and a half tall, and then he'd climb into my mind through my ear.

He only did it in awkward situations, like when I was talking to a pretty woman or handing in an essay, or something like that.

I told Doubt to knock it off, and he said I didn't really want him to, did I. He said he was only trying to help. I said how was it helping to creep into my mind after I'd handed in an essay, and he said he understood why I might think how I did. He said it was research for his PHD, though.

Doubt said right after I'd handed in an essay was the perfect time to creep into my mind, because it was safe, because he couldn't screw anything up. He promised that once he'd figured out how the human mind worked he'd help me get whatever I wanted.

After a while, I got suspicious of Doubt. He never wrote anything, or read anything except bad science fiction, and I hardly ever saw him on campus. I asked around and nobody'd ever heard of a PHD student named Doubt.

I had a job interview one afternoon in April. It was going really well and then they asked me a question that I wasn't sure how to answer. I paused for a moment and Doubt crept into my mind. He'd shrunk down beforehand and slipped into the pocket of my blazer and I hadn't even noticed.

I spotted Doubt on my shoulder, and I tried to stop him. I got hold of his foot as he was going for my ear. I pulled, but he got his shoe undone and it came off and he got inside my head.

One of the interviewers asked me why I had a doll's shoe in my hand, and I stuttered and then I said it was from one of my son's dolls.

One of the other interviewers flipped back through her notes and then she said "you have a son"? I said I didn't. I said I meant nephew, but she looked like she didn't believe me.

The interview got worse from there and I didn't get the job. I went to the bathroom before leaving and Doubt crept back out through my ear. He asked me where I'd put his shoe.

I said he'd cost me the job, and Doubt said it wasn't his fault. He said he'd tried his best and anyway, he didn't think it had gone that badly. I shoved Doubt and he shoved me back and I punched him in the face and his foot without the shoe slipped and he cracked his jaw on one of the bathroom sinks and he lost two teeth.

I moved out the next day, and I haven't seen Doubt since. Sometimes I still get this creeping feeling, though.

There was one night early on, where Doubt had this woman over. He wanted to show her the inside of my head. He begged me. He said if he could show her the inside of my head, he'd get laid for sure and he was happy and didn't nag after he got laid.

I said okay, and they shrunk down and crept into my mind. They were in there a while, long enough to plant a seed.

I started to think about that night, and I decided to track down Doubt and ask him about it. There's no trace of Doubt anywhere, though.

I've talked to a lot of people and they all give me weird looks and the private investigator took my money, but I'm pretty sure he hasn't done anything on my case.

Matryoshka

NADIA WAS THE GIRL HANGING OUT in the corner at Bob's party. Nadia was cute and she was dressed like a nineteenth century Russian peasant and she looked sad. I wasn't into the party, so I went and sat beside her.

Nadia said that she was Nadia, and I said that I was Jim. I said that she looked sad, and Nadia said that she was, and after she said that she was sad, I kissed her right on the mouth, which was a weird thing to do to a sad girl I didn't know.

Nadia smiled when I kissed her, but there was also a tear on her cheek. I went to wipe it away, and she took my hand and said let's leave, so we left. She led me through the dark for half an hour, until we got to the arboretum and then we sat under a willow tree and dangled our feet in the water. Nadia cried the whole time. Not sobs, just tears that streaked her mascara and somehow made her even cuter.

I said she was cute, especially with the streaked mascara, and she said I was sweet. I asked her what was wrong, and she said not to ruin the moment. She said talking about it wouldn't make it better, and if I wanted to do something I could kiss her again, or even put my hand up her dress, so I did both, and Nadia smiled again, although she kept crying.

We made love in the dark under the willow tree. An elderly couple walked by while it was happening. They stopped for a minute to watch, and then they kept going.

Afterwards, Nadia straightened her dress and I pulled up my pants and I walked her home. When we got to Nadia's place she didn't stop and turn around and say good night or anything, she just walked in and left the door open. I followed her in. Nadia's place was the ground floor of a house on Percy. It was nice, but it needed a paint job.

Nadia didn't say anything about my coming in, so I shut the door. I decided I'd stay until Nadia stopped crying, but she kept on. We lay down on her bed and she cried quietly while I kissed her cheeks and her neck and she fell asleep.

Nadia stopped crying when she fell asleep, and I was going to go, but it was two in the morning and I'd left my car at Bob's, so I stayed the night.

Nadia was already out of bed when I woke up. She was wearing jeans and a t-shirt and she was making pancakes. She wasn't crying, but she still looked sad. She smiled at me, and I kissed her and we ate pancakes. I said that I should go after breakfast, and Nadia said that I could go if I wanted to, but I shouldn't feel like I had to or anything. I said I'd stay if she wanted, but only if she'd tell me what she was sad about.

Nadia said that she was sad because she was solid. She said she'd felt solid for as long as she could remember, and her mom told her not to worry about it, but she did. She said she'd been to see someone last week and the tests had come back yesterday and they'd confirmed that she was solid.

I said what the hell did she mean, and she started to cry again. She said she knew I wouldn't understand, which is why she didn't tell me yesterday. She said nobody really understood how it was, not even her mom or her grandmother, and if you asked them about it, they'd tell you they were hollow inside and that that was just a part of life.

I said surely she didn't want to be hollow inside. Nadia said not yet maybe, but she'd never be hollow inside and that was a problem.

I didn't understand, but there was something about Nadia, and I went home to get my clothes and my toothbrush and then I stayed with her. She said she was glad. She said I made her happy. Nadia didn't seem happy, but she stopped crying and life was normal.

Nadia worked for a small IT firm in the market. Her mom and her grandmother lived in Toronto. Nadia's grandmother moved to Toronto from St Petersburg at the start of the Revolutionary War. Nadia didn't know any Russian when we met, but she started to study it as soon as she stopped crying. She said she wanted to see the motherland. She said she thought maybe she'd even take her mother and her grandmother with her.

Nadia finally explained the whole story to me after we'd been together for a year. She said her family were Matryoshka, and she was the last one in the line. She said that was what she meant about being solid. She said being the last one sucked, because the line depended on her in a way that it didn't with the others. All the others had to do was open their legs one time and get pregnant, but she had to reassemble the remains of all the others, and when she was done, she had to wait eight generations so that she could live another fifteen to thirty years or so. She said she'd never been old. She said she didn't even have the memory of being old like the others did.

I said how could she be a Matryoshka doll, and Nadia said she wasn't. She said her family had been Matryoshka long before there were dolls. She said the idea for the dolls came from her family. She said the guy who'd invented the dolls knew her great, great grandmother. He'd had an affair with her great, great grandmother and she'd told him the story of Nadia's family to reassure him that she couldn't get pregnant, because she already had a child and she was empty.

I said if Nadia wanted to grow old, why couldn't she? I said most people didn't get to live again and again like that, and lots of people were deciding not to have kids these days and letting their lines die out, and what was the big deal if another line died out? Nadia said she couldn't just grow old like that. She said it was her duty to gather the remains of the others. She said that was how it was, and she had to get on with it, because she was thirty now and she had no idea what happened after thirty. She said the memory of it was there and she'd only been as old as thirty one other time.

Nadia still waited another five years before going to Russia. At her grandmother's funeral, Nadia's mother pulled her aside and told her that she'd already waited too long, and now that her grandmother was dead and Nadia was thirty-five she'd better hurry up. Nadia said that her mother was right. She said she was at an uncharted age, and who knew how long it would last. She said she could get run over or something any day, and that would be the end of her family.

I said couldn't that have happened long ago? Nadia said maybe it could have, but it never had. She said all through her line everyone had one girl, and that was it, and nobody had ever died before having that one girl. She said when you considered pre-twentieth century infant mortality rates the only thing that made sense was that it was destiny. Nadia said if she left it too long though, she'd be too old to have a kid, even if she did collect the others. She said she was already past the ideal age for having kids.

Nadia left for Russia a few weeks after the funeral. She was gone two years. She wrote me all the time. She said she loved me and she hoped I'd wait for her, and I did.

When Nadia came back, she had six bags of bones and her mother. Nadia threw her arms around my neck and she kissed me and we made love and then she and her mother shut themselves up in the bedroom with the bones and there was lots of arguing in several different voices, sometimes in English and sometimes in Russian, and three days after it started, a woman came out.

The woman looked just like Nadia, except that she was seven inches taller and she was broader. The woman had a strong Russian accent. She said she was going to stay with me and that I should call her Nadia. She said Nadia had been gone for two years and people would assume she'd picked up the Russian accent while she was away, and she knew she was bigger than the old Nadia, but no one much would notice, because people didn't notice those things.

I said it was wrong how she and the rest of them had used Nadia. I said why couldn't Nadia live her life all the way through and grow old just once? The new Nadia sighed and said why couldn't she be young just once? She said look at her, she was thirty-seven, which was a lot of life behind her. She said that was just the way of things.

I stayed with the new Nadia. I didn't like her much, but she looked like the old Nadia and she had a lot of the same mannerisms, and sometimes, when I'd think about the old

Nadia and I'd cry, the new Nadia would hold me like it was something she understood from memory.

The new Nadia and I had a daughter. Nadia insisted on a Russian name, so we called her Irena.

I loved Irena. She was the spitting image of her mother, except that when she grew up she was an inch shorter and a dress size smaller. Irena was blissful. She didn't have the melancholy of the first Nadia, or the sternness of the second one.

I said so once to Nadia, and Nadia said of course she didn't. She said Irena was a long way from the end, which meant she wasn't even really conscious of being a Matryoshka and she wouldn't be until she was ready to have a child, and even then it wouldn't be the same as it was for her, or for the first Nadia.

Irena was so unconscious of it that when her mother died and I had her cremated and scattered her ashes, she didn't even say anything. Why would she? Her line won't die out for another six generations, with the first Nadia, who will finally get to grow old.

She Was Always There For Me

I WAS INTRODUCED TO MARTHA BY FONG, who was a friend of my brother. Martha was pretty and we got along, so I asked her out. We went out a few times and I really liked her. I told her I really liked her and she sighed and said, "Do we have to have this conversation now?"

I said we didn't, but I thought it was weird because she seemed like she liked me too. We kept going out. We had sex, and I stayed over at her place and she met my friends and I said, "I really like you," again, and after that I said, "I think I might even love you."

Martha sighed and said, "Are you sure?" and I said, "Yes, I'm sure. I love you Martha."

Martha said, "All right. Here's how it is. If you want me to, I'll love you for the rest of your life. I'll love you unconditionally. It won't matter what you do to me or anyone else, I'll love you, but I won't be there for you. I'll let you down constantly. When you need me by your side I'll be out at dinner with friends and I'll have my phone turned off, or I'll be in a meeting, or with another man and I won't come. Alternatively, I can be there for you whenever you need me. Your best and worst moments, I'll share them with you, but I won't love you."

I said that was a hell of a choice and she looked sheepish. "I know," she said.

I only half believed her, but I chose anyway. I said I'd rather have her there with me and Martha said that was a relief. "It's not that you're unlovable or that I'd be embarrassed to tell people that I love you or anything," she said. She said six guys and I was the first to choose having her there.

"I hurt them all and they hurt me. It was horrible the way I'd move in and out of their lives and how I'd let them down when they needed me. They all broke up with me and there was shouting and tears and I'd try to explain to them how it had to be, but they all just said if I really loved them."

I told her she didn't look old enough to have loved that many men that intensely. I asked her what had happened to them, and she said that they were dead.

I loved Martha anyway. Most of the time I couldn't even tell that she didn't love me. We went out places together and we fucked a lot and Martha always seemed like she enjoyed it. We got a place together, and sometimes we stayed in.

On holidays Martha came with me to my parents. I never met her family. I asked about them once, and Martha said she didn't have family. She said she didn't have friends either.

I was with Martha for three years, and then I started to notice how she'd be distracted when we were together. She stared off into space a lot. I asked her if she'd met somebody, and she said it didn't matter.

"I'll always be here for you," she said.

"But you don't love me," I said.

"I explained to you. I'm sorry," Martha said.

We split up and Martha got a place uptown, ten minutes by car. She said she didn't want to be too far in case I needed her.

"I'm done with that. I don't need you anymore," I said, but it wasn't true.

I tried to move on. I dated other women. I even moved in with one for a bit, but sometimes I needed Martha, and Martha was always there. Sometimes I'd go by her place and hang out and we'd fuck.

We both knew it wasn't the same as before, but she never seemed like she resented it. Even the night when I broke up with Cheryl and I showed up on the doorstep of Martha's apartment building at four in the morning, and there was this guy in the foyer with his shirt untucked and I'm pretty sure he'd just been with her.

I asked Martha about him, and she didn't say anything. She took my head and cradled it in her lap. Eventually we had sex. In the morning she called in sick for both of us and we slept until noon and then found a diner and had breakfast.

I got a promotion at work and somehow Martha knew. She showed up at my office and took me out to dinner to celebrate, and she used to go to the office Christmas parties when I didn't have another date.

When I got fired, Martha knew about that too. She was sitting on the steps outside my building waiting for me to come home. She took me out to dinner then too, and she stayed for three weeks.

When the doctors told me I was sick Martha held my hand. She came over every day with pizza or shawarma and we watched movies. When I didn't get better, she started to stay over again.

Martha was there when I died. She sat there with me on the floor of my apartment, but she seemed distracted. I said so.

"I'm sorry," she said and a tear slid down her cheek. "I've never done this before. I've loved people who've died and I haven't been there and that was terrible, but this is worse. I don't love you, and I've been seeing this other guy who I think I do love, and I'd really rather be at his place and I feel like such a phoney sitting here holding your hand. Why couldn't you have just let me love you like the rest?"

"It's okay Martha. I couldn't tell. Hardly ever," I said and I squeezed her hand.

She smiled a little bit and she looked at me earnestly. I had a feeling like she needed me to let her go, but she wasn't allowed to say it, like a curse in a fairy tale. I wondered if she needed someone to love her unconditionally too, no matter how often she let them down. I wondered if any of the five guys before me had loved her unconditionally after she'd let them down.

"Am I it? Are you done after me?" I said.

"Don't worry about me," she said.

I felt like I should tell her to leave, in case that would break the spell, but I said, "I'm glad you're here," and then I died.

Nancy's Photographs

NANCY HAD A PHOTOGRAPHIC MEMORY. Everything she'd ever seen in a series of snapshots. Her friends loved it. They'd go over to her place and they'd flip through her memory and it was better than an album, because the candid shots looked real.

Sometimes a friend would look at an old photo and say they'd sworn it hadn't happened like that, or that so and so wasn't there, but they knew the photographs didn't lie.

Nancy's friends and family took her on trips whenever they could, because who wants to fight with a camera when they're doing stuff, and besides Nancy was fun to hang out with.

Nancy didn't mind it. Her friends and family always paid her airfare and sometimes they paid for her hotels and food too.

The only time it was a pain was after the vacation when people would get together and they'd spend the evening eating finger foods and flipping through Nancy's memory with their greasy hands, but Nancy never said anything. She liked having a photographic memory and the attention she got for it.

Lately, Nancy had started to feel like the technology of her memory was outdated, though. The photos just sat there one after the other. Some of them were underexposed and some were overexposed and sometimes somebody had a big pimple or a stain on their shirt, and they'd look at her like what the hell did she leave that in for, but she couldn't help it.

Nancy couldn't edit photos. She couldn't delete them either. She had a few photos that she didn't want people to see, because she was thirty-four after all. She kept those photos pretty well grouped and steered people away from them, but sometimes one or two got seen.

Nancy had to be especially careful on vacation, because everybody wanted to see those photos. It cost Nancy a boyfriend back in college. She was showing pictures of a trip to Barcelona. There were all these photos of the ass of this guy she walked behind through Parc Guell, and her boyfriend got pissed off and broke up with her over it.

Nancy didn't do anything about it until after Kerry's boyfriend came over one night and they fucked. Kerry's boyfriend was hot and they had a few drinks and they made out and then he tied her face down to the bed frame.

When Kerry came over, she saw the photos and she gave Nancy a bloody nose.

After that Nancy went to see a guy she'd heard about on the internet. He lived in a room in a basement near Jane and Finch and he wanted thirty grand. Nancy sold her condo to get the money.

The guy knew what he was doing. He changed it so Nancy could edit and delete photos she didn't like, and so she could offload them so people wouldn't keep going through her memory all the time.

Nancy retouched the photos of Kerry's boyfriend, and then she showed them to Vanessa. Nancy said she was embarrassed by the photos, and she wouldn't have shown Vanessa, but she felt she had to, because you could see the resemblance to Kerry's boyfriend, but clearly it wasn't him.

Vanessa told Kerry, and Kerry said she knew what she'd seen. Vanessa said Kerry should take another look, so she did. Kerry couldn't find her boyfriend, or even ropes and afterwards she made up with both her boyfriend and Nancy.

Kerry's boyfriend wouldn't go back to Kerry though, and one night he went to Nancy's. He told Nancy that he liked Kerry, but he wasn't in love with her, and then he said he'd never had sex like that night.

Nancy said like which night, and Kerry's boyfriend said she knew which night. Nancy said she didn't, and then Kerry's boyfriend went all through Nancy's memory and he couldn't find the photos and he had to concede it hadn't happened. He'd been drunk, and photographs don't lie.

Not Young Anymore

THIS GUY CAME UP TO ME in the middle of the street and told me I wasn't young anymore. I asked him who the hell he thought he was, and he shrugged and walked away.

I told all my friends about it, and they said they figured they were young enough. My sister too, and she's three years older than me and she's married and has a kid.

"How the fuck can that be?" I said, and my sister said it was just some guy on the street and I shouldn't take it seriously.

I couldn't help it though. I lost sleep over it. I told my dad about it and he said, yeah, come to think of it he'd noticed it lately. There was a certain quality, he said. "It happens. It happened to me and your mother too. You were eight when it happened to me. You remember when I ran off with Shelley from the office for three weeks?" my dad said.

"Yeah but you were forty-two when I was eight. I'm only thirty-one and Mary's thirty-four and," I said. My dad said he didn't know what to tell me.

I saw the same guy downtown a couple of weeks later and I cornered him. I asked him what the hell he'd meant, I wasn't young anymore, and he said he thought it was pretty self-explanatory.

I pressured him and he told me there was a department responsible for deciding these things and they'd decided that I wasn't young anymore.

"How? Look at me. I'm not going grey, or bald and my skin's good," I said, and he said, "It's not really about that." "I don't have kids, either, or a wife. I don't own a house. I barely have a job. How am I not still young?" I said. He said he didn't know.

I asked him at what age people stopped being young and he said it varied. "On average," I said. "It varies. It depends on what part of the world, all kinds of stuff. In Canada I'd say they usually stop being young somewhere in their early forties," he said.

"I'm only thirty-one. Why am I not young anymore?" I said. "It's best not to ask those sorts of questions," he said, but I kept pressuring him so he told me.

"It's like an economics thing. It's kind of a measure of what you've achieved versus what you're expected to achieve," he said.

"Are you saying I've got no potential?" I said. He said it wasn't just up to him, but anyway it was complicated. "There are a lot of factors go into it. We review the evidence pretty carefully," he said. He said I could appeal if I wanted, but most people didn't have much luck. "We review the evidence pretty carefully," he said again.

He said it wasn't so bad, not being young anymore, but he obviously felt guilty about it because he bought me a coffee. He bought me a brownie too and we sat and talked about women. Before he left, he gave me a card. He said if I wanted to appeal the decision I should call the number on the card and ask for Charlie. He said they don't overturn decisions very often, though, and on my way home, I chucked the card in the garbage, because I know I don't have a case.

Meat Trucks in Heaven

HEAVEN WAS AWESOME AT FIRST. Mostly I lay out in the sun and ate and drank. I lay out without sunscreen, but I never got a burn because you don't get burns in heaven. Sometimes I got hot, though, and I'd get off my chair and go for a swim and the water was always perfect.

They took care of everything for you in heaven. It was like a five star resort, but better. When I came back from swimming there was always somebody holding a towel for me. People showed up with plates of food whenever I wanted, and the people were always well dressed and attractive and friendly.

The great thing was I could eat and eat and I never felt sick or got heartburn or anything. It was the same thing with drinking. You could get a pleasant buzz, but you never got nauseous or hungover.

The sex in heaven was amazing too. Whenever you were in the mood, a bunch of beautiful women and men would come by and stand in front of you, and you could pick as many of them as you wanted and they'd just go off with you and do whatever you wanted.

Moira, who was a neighbour of mine back in the seventies, was there and sometimes we'd sit and eat and drink and talk about how great heaven was.

I started to get these weird feelings about it all, though. I noticed Moira was putting on weight from all the food and alcohol, and then I noticed that I was too. I didn't feel any different, but I looked fat.

I started to think about the young women I fucked, and how they were perfect in every detail, and how if I were them I wouldn't want to fuck a fat, middle-aged man.

I did callisthenics in the mornings, but I hated doing them and I couldn't lose weight anyway with all the food I ate, and then I started to think about the people who brought me the food, and the drinks and the towels and did my laundry and stuff. They were all over. There were all these people in heaven doing shit for me.

These people were in heaven too, but they worked all hours of the day and night. I talked to one man and he said they did shift work. He said mostly it wasn't too bad, but they were always on call in case things were busier than expected, and if you got called in on your day off or something, that really sucked.

After that, I decided to cook all my own food and serve it myself and do the dishes afterwards. I invited Moira over for dinner one night, and she said why would I make dinner when my food wasn't as good as heaven's.

I stuck with it anyway. Every morning people dropped off what I wanted fresh, and I started to think about how people were still doing work for me.

Anytime I fucked a woman, I asked her if she enjoyed it. She always said sure, but I couldn't believe it. "You're so beautiful, though," I always said and they shrugged.

I asked Moira if she knew where all these people had come from and Moira said she didn't think about it. "Do you think those beautiful young men enjoy fucking you?" I said. Moira got pissed. She said what was I implying and then she called for some men and she went away with two of them.

I called some women and picked one, but I couldn't fuck her. I kept looking at my belly and thinking about how disgusting she must find me.

I asked the woman who she worked for, and she said she wasn't a whore, unless I wanted her to be. I said I didn't. I said I just wanted to know who was in charge in heaven.

The woman said was I sure I wanted to know that? I said yes, and she said she didn't think I did. I said I really did, and she took me to an office and a woman in scrubs came out and led me away.

The woman in scrubs had me do some paperwork, and then she sent me to a boot camp to get in shape. After the boot camp, I was given a job doing meat deliveries. I'm at the slaughterhouse at five and I can hear the screams as they kill the animals, and some guys load up the back of my truck and then I drive it around to different resorts and to one or two people who prefer to make their own food.

I quit after a week and went back to the resort, but I only lasted three days there, because I kept thinking about how now somebody else had to do my job.

My supervisor said, yeah, that was how it was. "Once you start to think like that, it's too late," he said.

One day I had to deliver meat to Moira. She said what was I doing, and I said I was doing deliveries now. Moira said she'd been thinking about what I'd said and maybe I had a point. I said I didn't have a point and I put the meat on the counter and left.

The Old Drunk at the Bar

MY MOM WAS IN A BAR ONE NIGHT and this old drunk came up and hit on her. He told her he was an angel, "an archangel actually," he said, and my mom, who wasn't born yesterday, told him to prove it.

He was drunk and he was indiscreet and he said sure he'd prove it. "What if I could tell you something about yourself that I couldn't know," he said. My mom said she might believe him, and he told her about how she'd had a daughter thirteen months before me who'd been stillborn.

My mom said that didn't prove it. She said there weren't a lot of people who knew about that, but it only took one to spread it around. She said if the angel could make it so her daughter had lived, that would prove it.

The angel, who was actually an archangel, was drunk and he was indiscreet and he asked my mom if she'd go to bed with him if he could make it so her daughter had lived. "If you can make that happen, I'll sleep with you," my mom said.

The archangel made it happen, and my mom slept with him and now I don't exist. It turns out that since my parents already had a kid, they didn't feel a rush to do it again. My little sister still exists. She's a year and a half older than she was before, but apparently that was close enough.

My older sister has done well for herself. She has a PHD in physics and she holds a research chair at Cambridge and she's not even forty. It's rubbed off on my little sister too. Before, she was working at a restaurant downtown and going to school part-time. Now she's a concert pianist. She's performed all over Europe and the US and people say she's a genius.

Nobody knows anything about what happened, except my mom, who's pleased as punch, because I made twelve bucks an hour doing demolitions and apparently I dragged everyone down with me.

The angel got in a lot of shit for the whole thing. Apparently angels aren't supposed to do stuff like that. The angel used to be an archangel and now he's not. Now he doesn't even have wings. He genuinely seems to feel bad about what happened, though. He's trying to make amends, but he's a drunk.

He calls at four in the morning all the time to say how sorry he is. He's always drunk when he does it. He says he just wasn't thinking, and my mom may be older, but she still does that to a guy.

I'm not really pissed at the angel anymore, or at the situation, just depressed. It seems the world really is better off without me. My family definitely is, and I can't stop thinking about that. That's why I'm always awake at four in the morning when the angel calls and it's why I always pick up, even though I know he's drunk.

The Best Day of Jerry's Life

IT TOOK JERRY UNTIL JUST AFTER TEN in the morning to realize he was having the best day of his life. Jerry'd had some shitty days and a lot of mediocre days and even a few good days and he knew what was going on.

It wasn't Jerry's birthday or Christmas or his wedding day or the day his kid was born, or any of the other shit people think of when they think of the best day of their lives. It was just a normal day, except everything went right.

Jerry felt good when he woke up. He got in the shower and the temperature was perfect, and he spent what felt like a long time in there, but he still had plenty of time when he got out. On his way to work he found a twenty on the sidewalk, and then he ran into Tom at the coffee shop and he hadn't seen Tom in months and Tom insisted on buying.

At ten they came into Jerry's office and told him his boss, who was a dick, was leaving. They said they wanted Jerry to take over his boss' position. They said there really wasn't anyone else, and also that meant meetings in Paris next month.

Jerry called me after that. He said he was suspicious. I said about what, and he said he thought he was having the best day of his life. I said that was awesome, but I was busy and were we still on for drinks later. Jerry said it wasn't awesome, but we were still on for drinks.

Jerry met a woman at lunch. He bumped into her at the hotdog cart downstairs and spilled her drink. The woman was really cute and she wasn't pissed at all about the drink and she even asked Jerry to go to dinner with her.

The day kept going like that. There was a power outage in Jerry's building and everyone got sent home at two.

I met Jerry for drinks at five-thirty. He'd just come from the beach he said. Jerry looked frazzled. I said he didn't look a guy who was having the best day of his life, and Jerry said trust him, he was.

He said it was no good having the best day of his life, though. He said he was only thirty-three and what the hell was that? He said he didn't want to spend the rest of his life thinking about how the best day of his life was done with, and given life expectancies these days he could expect to spend at least the next fifty years, and maybe the next sixty or seventy years, thinking about it.

He said it would be one thing if it was subtle, but this was way over the top. He said it would be how the best day of your life would be if it was a reality show.

He said if nothing happened, he'd end up fucking this woman after dinner, and she'd be kinky and really tight and Jesus, what was he going to do.

I told Jerry to shut up. I told him he should enjoy the day. I said he could be wrong about it being the best day of his life. I said it was a good day, but you never knew. I said tomorrow could be even better and what about getting married say, or having kids.

Jerry said I didn't know, because I hadn't lived it. He said if I'd lived it I'd understand. The whole day. It was relentless he said.

I told Jerry to stand the woman up then. He said he didn't think that would work. He said he couldn't sabotage the best day of his life. He said I could though. He said I could show up and make a complete ass of myself and scare her off for him.

I said he was out of his mind and I wasn't doing that, but I did do it. I showed up ten minutes into Jerry's date, before the appetizers even. I acted drunk and I talked really loudly and I grabbed the woman's breast and that did it.

Jerry said he couldn't believe I'd grabbed her breast, but thanks for that. He said she was turning out to be kind of a bitch, and maybe I was right that he wasn't having the best day of his life after all.

Then the waitress came over. She said she was so sorry and his food was on the house and then she threw me out.

Jerry called me at eleven. He said he was at the waitress' place. He said she was fucking incredible. He said she was a Masters student and she was really smart and really interesting. He said he'd told her about how he thought he was having the best day of his life, and about earlier at the restaurant. He said she understood.

According to the coroner's report Jerry died shortly after twelve as the result of an accident in the shower.

Cloud Nine

MY BROTHER AND HIS WIFE bought a condo on Cloud Nine. Cloud Nine was a big cumulus cloud off the coast near San Diego. The condo was expensive as hell, but my brother and his wife do pretty well.

There were issues with the construction, because building on clouds is still pretty new, so my brother and his wife moved in with me until their condo was ready.

My brother's wife complained that my place was shit. She said how could I live like that at my age and my brother said don't worry, it wouldn't be for long.

My brother and his wife stayed at my place for eight months and they didn't pay rent. They didn't even buy groceries or anything.

When they moved out, my brother slapped me on the back and said I was welcome on Cloud Nine anytime I wanted to drop by. My brother's wife gave my brother a look, like she didn't want me hanging out at their place on Cloud Nine, but I went anyway. My brother's condo was fairly small, because he and his wife do pretty well, but Cloud Nine was really expensive.

Cloud Nine was gorgeous. Everything was walkable and there were shuttles to and from the Earth that came every three minutes that didn't make any noise. There was security you had to get past, but they didn't hassle you if you were supposed to be there.

My brother and his wife were happy as shit on Cloud Nine until it turned out that it wasn't Cloud Nine at all.

The developers who owned Cloud Nine, and also Cloud Six, which is where they built, decided to pull a fast one. It turned out that the real Cloud Nine was a nimbus cloud near the arctic over Norway and it was a good bit smaller than Cloud

Six, so the developers swapped the numbers and hoped no one noticed.

The developers claimed it didn't matter. They said the cloud was Paradise, and a six was just a nine upside down, but people didn't agree and the bottom dropped right out of the Cloud Six real estate market. The day after the news broke, the value of my brother's condo dropped from twelve million to two-hundred thousand. My brother and his wife were stuck with a huge mortgage on a property that was almost worthless.

Problems started cropping up on Cloud Six too. A lot of people sold off and a bad element moved in and it wasn't safe to go out at night anymore.

Then they had problems with the shuttles. The noiseless technology broke down and they had to replace the shuttles with helicopters which only came every hour and made a shitload of noise.

My brother and his wife sold off their condo and moved back in with me. They're suing the developer like everybody else who bought a place when they thought it was Cloud Nine.

My brother said it wouldn't be long. He said the developer would be forced to settle and then he and his wife could buy a place and they'd be out of my hair. I said why would the developer settle, and then I said even if they did settle, it could take years and my brother and his wife should rent a place.

My brother said he wasn't about to rent, because renting was just throwing money away, so I went and gave my landlord my notice. I took a leave from work and I'm going to travel for a bit. My brother and his wife say that's great, but where are they supposed to live?

Carpe Diem

I SEIZED THE DAY. I got him coming out of the shower and threw him against the wall and I slapped the handcuffs on him, before he had a chance to grab a towel even.

I'd never seized a day before, but I was desperate, because I had a big meeting with a client and I wasn't good at big meetings with clients.

I tried to beg off the meeting. I said let Hoenecker handle it. I said Hoenecker was good at those sorts of things.

My boss said Hoenecker was good at those sorts of things, but Hoenecker wasn't in, and it was part of my job after all, and what was I good at? She said money was tight and if we didn't sign the client, she wasn't sure how we were going to pay my salary.

I called Hoenecker about it, and he said to seize the day. I said what did he mean, and he said my problem was that I was a pussy. He said every time we went for drinks for example. He said every time we went for drinks I moaned about how I didn't have a girlfriend, but I never approached anyone. He said seize the day. "At least once in your life, seize the day, goddammit," he said.

In The Day's bathroom, The Day said how the hell did I get in there. I told him I'd walked in. I said the door wasn't locked and Last Night was passed out drunk on the couch.

The Day said what a fucker Last Night was. He said he should have known better than to trust him. He said it was Last Night's job to keep watch until The Day left for work. "He's supposed to wait until I'm dressed and have my coffee at least," The Day said.

I told The Day he could take it up with Last Night later. I said right now I had him and I needed his help. The Day said why did he give a shit if some two-bit loser like me needed his help, and I said because I had the keys to the handcuffs.

The Day said if that was the case, could I loosen them a bit, because they were pinching his wrists. I said too bad. I said if he helped me out like I needed, I'd take them right off.

The Day said there was nothing he'd love more, but he couldn't help me. I told him I knew better. I said I knew he had a complete database of everything that was supposed to happen during his shift and I wanted to see it.

The Day said I was right about the database, but the database was huge. He said it covered seven billion people's interactions, not to mention all the plants and animals in the world and even if he found my file and changed it, he'd have to change thousands, maybe millions of others and then he had to write a separate report for each one.

I told The Day maybe he wouldn't need to do a report. I said it depended on how things went for me that afternoon. I said for now I just wanted to see.

The Day said he couldn't do it. He said it would take months to scroll through the database to find the relevant entry. I said surely the database was searchable and my name used Latin characters and that should eliminate a few billion people right there.

The Day said fine, he'd look into it, but not dripping wet with his prick dangling loose. I towelled The Day off and got him some shorts. The Day said that would do, because he had a computer downstairs that could do what he needed, but he wanted a coffee first.

I made The Day a coffee and I held it up to his lips while he drank. He complained that it wasn't strong enough or hot enough, and I said could we get down to it already.

The Day said what was the rush? He said it was still early and nothing much would happen for a bit, but I wasn't buying it. I grabbed The Day's laptop and booted it up and told him I wanted to see my file.

The Day said how was he going to do anything with his hands cuffed behind his back, so I undid the cuffs and redid them in front. The Day said great, now what was my name again? I told him and he said brilliant, there couldn't be more than a few thousand of those and was he supposed to go through them all?

I seized The Day by the throat and told him to figure it out and quick. I gave him my birth date and where I was born and said that should do it, shouldn't it. The Day gasped that he couldn't breathe and then he gasped that he'd cooperate and I let go of his throat.

The Day pulled up my file and there was my big meeting with the clients. The database said I didn't sign the clients. I told The Day he was going to write in a change, that the clients were going to sign. I said while he was at it, he was going to set me up with a date for dinner with the woman from the law firm in the building next door.

The Day said how was he supposed to do that? I said we could bump into each other in the coffee shop on the way to my pitch. "Figure something out. It's not rocket science," I said. The Day said of course it wasn't rocket science, but that didn't mean it wasn't complicated. He said what was her name, and what if she wasn't free? He said he was going to end up messing with a lot of files.

I told The Day I didn't know her name, but if he went through everyone who worked in the firm, I could pick her out, so he did.

It took The Day four hours, but he did it all. I watched him. The Day said that was it, now let him go, but I didn't.

I said I wasn't stupid. I said as soon as I let The Day go, he'd change everything back to how it had been. The Day swore he wouldn't. He said that was way more work than he wanted to do and he didn't even remember how it had read before, but I wasn't taking a chance.

I drugged The Day and shoved him into the trunk of my car and took him back to my place, where I tied him up tightly and gagged him and threw him in the hall closet.

The meeting with the clients went brilliantly. They signed after just twenty minutes.

The lawyer at the firm next door was Marcie. We had a nice dinner and we wound up back at her place. Around eleven,

I told her I had to go. She asked me to stay the night, and I said I'd love to, but I had a big meeting tomorrow morning.

I let The Day go when I got home. I told him how everything had gone beautifully. I said thanks for everything. The Day said I could go fuck myself. He said he'd been warned that sometimes people seized Days, but he'd never really believed it.

On the way out, he said he'd get me back, but we both knew there was nothing he could do, because Tonight had taken over and Tomorrow was another Day.

The Emotional State

LOVE CONQUERED ALL. Love did it by taking the long view. By the time anyone realized what was happening, it was too late.

Religion dominated for a long time, but there were always challengers. Intolerance and Despair rode hard on Religion's heels, and Self-Interest was a perennial force, but Love moved forward a bit at a time, and the others started to lose their grip. People took to marrying for love, and then they started leaving marriages for love. They showered their kids with love. They even showered their pets with love.

When they saw what was happening, the other emotions tried to block Love. The less important emotions were afraid of a coalition between Religion and Self-Interest, so they tried to promote Understanding. Understanding was backed by Acceptance and Justice and Happiness, but also by Hatred and Bitterness and Rage, who recognized the danger. The coalition might have worked, but Intolerance and Religion and Self-Interest worked to undermine Understanding, and the group collapsed.

Once Love had conquered all, it strangled debate. It censored the press. No expressions of Hatred or Anger could get through. Love even silenced Compassion and Joy who had been supporters of Love since the early days.

It wasn't a violent coup. Love came to power quietly, gradually marginalizing everything else until it had complete control.

People didn't fight Love's regime, because they assumed that Love would preside over a hedonistic paradise, but that hasn't happened. In order to secure its conquest, Love destroyed all the institutions that could challenge it, and left everyone so besotted that industry and agriculture collapsed and society ceased to function.

Hatred and Bitterness spoke out. They started up Samizdat, like back in Soviet times, to get around the censorship. Love published responses to these illegal presses, and then it shut them down, and nobody heard from Hatred or Bitterness again. Gradually the rest were silenced too, and Love's conquest was complete.

People are starving under Love's regime. They live in squalor while the world crumbles around them. They're not happy about it, although they're not exactly pissed either. They live the life Love chooses for them, and they don't question it.

Falling In Love

ME AND JIMMY AND AHMED were really tight going back to high school. When Jimmy was going to get married to Lucy, Ahmed was going to be the best man and I was going to be right beside Ahmed. The whole thing fell through though, and after that Ahmed didn't hang out with me and Jimmy anymore.

Jimmy saw Lucy one day on a bus that was going by, and he fell in love on the spot. I was there. Jimmy got this look in his eye and he took off after the bus. He ran for a block banging on the side of it to try and get the bus driver to stop. Lucy looked out the window at him and he smiled at her and waved.

The bus didn't stop for Jimmy, but it got stuck at the light and Jimmy and I got to the next stop before it did. When we got on, the driver gave Jimmy shit for banging on the side of his bus, like he owned it and not the city.

Jimmy didn't have any bus tickets or any money and all I had was a twenty, so we had to give the bus driver that. Jimmy went straight up to Lucy and told her he'd never seen anyone like her and he was in love. Lucy was impressed enough to go to dinner with Jimmy and then they became a couple.

The thing was, Lucy wasn't the first girl Jimmy'd tried that on. He was always doing it. Sometimes he'd approach three or four women in a day and he'd tell them all that he'd never seen anyone like them and that he was in love. It never worked until Lucy, though.

Ahmed said it burned him up. He said it was a dirty way to meet women. "Nobody can really fall in love all the time like that. Jimmy's just a horny prick. Watch, I bet he'll be sick of Lucy in a week," Ahmed said.

Ahmed never said that to Jimmy, but Jimmy knew. He said once that he felt like Ahmed thought he was full of shit when he'd say he was in love with all these women. He said he felt like Ahmed was jealous too. "I think he's got a thing for Lucy," he said.

Ahmed did have a thing for Lucy. It got stronger the longer she was with Jimmy. "I can't stand that he's with her. You and Jimmy are my best friends, but you know she's too good for him. God man, she's too good for any of us, really. She's fucking perfect man," he said.

Then a week before the wedding Jimmy and Lucy broke up. Jimmy said they were having lunch at that new place on Bank Street when she freaked out on him. She said she knew that he hadn't really loved her that day, that it was just a stupid ploy he used to meet women. Jimmy said that wasn't true, but even if it was, he obviously loved her now. She said that wasn't obvious at all. She said how did she know he wasn't still running after buses, and even if he did love her now it was too late. Then she stormed out and left him with the cheque.

Jimmy was heartbroken. He was pissed too. "It had to be Ahmed," he said to me. "Only you and Ahmed know I used to try that to get girls. Ahmed always thought it was cheating, and I saw the way he looked at Lucy. That son-of-a-bitch," Jimmy said to me.

It didn't help that six days after they broke up Jimmy went over to Lucy's at two in the morning and Ahmed was sitting on the balcony in his boxers reading a magazine. After that Ahmed didn't hang out with me and Jimmy anymore.

A month after Jimmy found Ahmed on the balcony, Ahmed showed up at my door. He said he broke it off with Lucy. He said she wasn't as perfect as he always thought. I told him to come in, and I gave him a beer. "You did it, didn't you," Ahmed said. I told him I didn't, and he said I had to have, because he sure as hell didn't do it and nobody else was around Jimmy enough to know how he was.

Jimmy started chasing women again around the same time. Everywhere we'd go Jimmy would spot a woman and say he was madly in love, and we'd follow her around. Somehow it wasn't the same without Ahmed around, so I tried to talk Jimmy into making up with him. "He swears he didn't tell Lucy," I said.

"Of course he does. He's a lying fucking snake. I couldn't believe you forgave him after what he did with Sandy. I know how much you loved her. And then he did it again to me. Even if he didn't tell her, he still fucked her afterwards and maybe during, like he did with Sandy."

Jimmy met Emma a couple of months later. He was walking by a shoe store and he saw her in there trying on a pair of black slingbacks. He went in and told her he'd never seen anyone so beautiful and then he asked her if she believed in love at first sight.

Jimmy and Emma lasted about a year. Then she dumped him. Jimmy said she started going on about Lucy and how he'd pulled the same kind of shit with her and how he pulled it with any woman he thought was hot, and what was it just some kind of game he played.

Jimmy asked me if I'd told her. I said no, but I might have hesitated. Anyway, Jimmy called me a liar. He said Sandy wasn't his fault and it had been three years and I needed to move on.

"Find some woman and fall in love again goddammit. It's not my fault it's easy for me. I know you and Ahmed never believed me, but I really do fall in love with all these women," Jimmy said.

Actually, I always believed Jimmy. I believed Ahmed too when he said he was in love with Sandy and Lucy. I don't think either of them could help it. I'm jealous of that.

I told everyone I was in love with Sandy. I even told Sandy that, but I wasn't. I've never been in love. Not even a little. I think maybe I can't fall in love. That's why I told Lucy and Emma about Jimmy. I'm not secretly in love with Jimmy or anything, it's just that when your friends are in love they don't have so much time for you, and if you can't fall in love, you need friends who are around all the time.

We don't hang out anymore, any of us. I ran into Ahmed at a Starbucks a while back. He said Jimmy got married and he seems to love her. Ahmed loves her too. He fucks her when Jimmy's not around, but it's more than that. "I think she loves us both, to be honest man," Ahmed said.

Ahmed asked about me, if I'd met anyone. I told him yeah. I told him I'd been out with a couple of girls. I told him the last one was pretty serious, but she'd broken my heart and now I was taking a break from it all. I think he bought it.

Cupid

THE OLD GUY ACROSS THE STREET saw Cupid sitting on Olivia's roof and called the cops and the cops came down and picked Cupid up.

I knew Olivia from the time I was thirteen. I had a crush on her all through high school, but we never hooked up. After high school we went away different places for university and I forgot about Olivia for a bit. Then I saw her on the subway and she hadn't aged at all. I sat down across from her and I smiled at her. I even bumped into her when I got up and said sorry, but she didn't say anything back.

It sucked that Olivia ignored me, because she was really hot. I told my friends about her. I told them I'd had a crush on her in high school and how if anything she was even hotter now, and they said why didn't I say anything to her. I said next time for sure I'd say something.

I rode the same subway at the same time everyday hoping to see Olivia again. I even did see her once, but she was at the far end of the car and it was crowded and I couldn't get over to talk to her.

I told Mark, and Mark said Jesus I was a pussy. He said if I was serious why didn't I ride the subway until she got off, or push my way through the car to get to her. He said women liked that sort of thing. I said no they didn't, and he said she wasn't just going to fall in love with me, and the next day he sent me a link to Cupid's website.

I didn't even know Cupid was still around, but according to his website he was around and taking contracts. The website had details about how it worked, testimonials from clients, even a fee structure. I sent Cupid an email about Olivia and he called me up. He said he could make Olivia fall in love with me if I wanted. He said the case sounded pretty routine.

Cupid charged a fair bit for his services. He said he knew it sounded crass charging money for that sort of thing, but these days it was harder to live like a god. He said people didn't sacrifice the way they used to, and when the bank had foreclosed on his house in '06 he'd had to start taking clients.

Cupid said it would cost fifteen grand to get Olivia to fall in love with me. I said that seemed like a lot of money, and Cupid said you get what you pay for. He said there were lots of scammers out there promising love potions and stuff, but he was the real deal. He said he'd take care of everything. He said I didn't need to be there to make it happen. He said we'd meet up before, and he'd get a blood sample and that was all he needed from me.

Cupid said if I was really concerned about cost, he'd do it for ten grand the week after Valentine's Day. He said the two weeks before Valentine's Day were the busiest of the entire year, but between Valentine's and Easter work was always dead.

Then the old guy across the street from Olivia called the cops, and the cops came and picked Cupid up before he had a chance to shoot her. I went down to see Cupid at the lockup, and he bitched about how they'd taken his bow and arrow and they'd made him put on clothes and the clothes were way too big, because look at him, he was barely three feet, and they put him in denim and the denim chafed.

I asked Cupid why he didn't just shoot the cops when they came for him, and he said with what. "Do you want the cops to fall in love with you?" he said. He said anyway it wasn't a big deal, he'd do it when he got out.

I talked to Cupid's lawyer and he said it might be a while before Cupid got out. He said the law frowned on guys in diapers who wandered around the city with bows and arrows stalking young women.

The lawyer said the court was sending Cupid for a psych test and he wasn't sure Cupid would pass.

I told the lawyer I didn't really care about any of that. I told him I just wanted my money back. I said Cupid may have given me a discount, but his fee wasn't exactly low. I said I'd had to max out my credit card and borrow five grand from my mom and Cupid hadn't delivered. The lawyer said okay, if that was how I wanted it, but the law also frowned on people who hired guys in diapers to shoot women through the heart with arrows.

Cupid made bail, but the bow and arrow were impounded as evidence. The case went to trial and the lawyer painted the cops as culturally insensitive. He said how in Ancient Greece cherubs were supposed to go around in diapers, or even naked, and Cupid wasn't doing anything illegal by wandering around in a diaper which was properly secured and unsoiled. He said at worst Cupid was guilty of trespassing. Cupid was acquitted, but the whole thing took a year and a half.

It turned out Olivia'd had a boyfriend. He'd asked her to marry her on Valentine's Day, right before Cupid was supposed to shoot her, and she'd said yes and by the time Cupid was acquitted, Olivia was married.

Cupid followed through on the contract anyway. He sent me a card in the mail covered in hearts that said thinking of you. Inside he said sorry for the delay. Olivia called me up a couple of weeks later. I asked her where she'd gotten my number, and she said it wasn't hard, and now I see Olivia whenever she can.

Olivia says she won't leave her husband for me. She says it's not fair to her husband, and she has a lot more in common with him than she does with me, and anyway she can't see us like that. She says lets face it, we'd be a disaster together. It makes me sad when she says that, but then she says she loves me, and she goes down on me, and it's better.

Down the Hall

MIKE'S NEIGHBOUR DOWN THE HALL, who was retired and bored, told Mike about this place in the mall that his cousin owned. The neighbour said his cousin took in unwanted gold for new memories. "You're always fingering that ring, ever since you moved in. You should take it to him and tell him I sent you. He'll give you a good deal. By the way, I'm Bruce and my cousin's Arkell."

Mike went to the mall one night. He walked by the store a couple of times and it looked kind of dingy. There was a sign on a post in the doorway that said, "Trade in your unwanted gold for new memories," and it had two pictures. The one on the left had a guy with a wedding ring crying. The one on the right had the same guy without the ring running through long grass with two kids and a dog.

Mike went into the HMV next door and bought a copy of *Who Framed Roger Rabbit*. He came back out and looked at the sign for a couple of seconds and then he walked in and put the ring on the counter.

"She left you?" this fat guy with a bulbous nose said.

"Yeah. Are you Arkell?" Mike said and Arkell said sure he was. Mike said that Bruce had told him about the place and Arkell said, "Huh? How do you like that? How is that old bastard?" Mike shrugged and Arkell shrugged and then Arkell picked up the ring.

"Ten karats," Arkell said.

"We were young. We didn't have any money then," Mike said.

"I can't give you too much for ten karats. Probably I can fix up the end for you a little, but that's it. I don't suppose she left behind any earrings or an engagement ring or anything, eh?" Arkell said.

"No."

"Well, if you find any other gold lying around, we can always modify your memories again, or expand on what we've already changed. For now, these are what you're looking at," Arkell said. He pulled out a huge book and opened it to page one hundred and twelve. Arkell grabbed a handful of pages. "From there to there."

The book had options for new memories. There was one where she'd died, and one where Mike had broken up with her, and another where the whole thing never happened. Mike pointed at the last one and said, "That's it. That's the one I want."

Arkell said Mike didn't really want that one. "I don't even know why we make it an option for endings," he said. "It really only works if you get rid of all of it. If you just delete the ending then you're left with unfinished business. You'll end up calling her at four AM wondering why the hell she hasn't come home yet."

"I want it all gone, then," Mike said. Arkell said that was fine, but not for one ring that was a lousy ten karats, no matter Arkell's cousin referred him. Mike asked him what it would take. Arkell said a fair bit, and he doubted a guy who came in with a wedding ring that was only ten karats could put together that kind of a collection.

"Do you ever see her around?" Arkell said. "No, she moved back east," Mike said, and Arkell said in that case Mike should just have her killed off. "In your memories of course. I don't run that kind of outfit, but if she's dead in your mind then you've got closure and all that."

Mike said he'd have to think about it, but he went back two days later and did it. It was horrible. Everywhere Mike went he thought he saw Rebecca, and he cried himself to sleep each night. He thought about the fight they'd had a couple of days before, the one that led her to drive back east to see her parents and ended up with her car going off a cliff in the fog.

Bruce saw Mike in the hallway a few mornings later, and Mike had just been crying. Bruce slapped him on the back and told him things'd get better. "But if they don't, my cousin runs a shop in the mall. His name's Arkell. Just go in there and tell him I sent you," Bruce said.

Mike went to the shop. He told Arkell his wife had died and he couldn't sleep at night and he'd heard that Arkell took old jewellery for new memories. Arkell said yeah, it was true. He said he'd love to help out and what did Mike have. Mike shrugged and Arkell said he was running a business here and he had to eat same as everyone else.

Mike went and asked his mom if she had any gold she didn't want anymore. "Who doesn't want gold?" she said. Mike shrugged and sat on her couch and skimmed the newspaper until she went out for groceries. Then he went upstairs to her jewellery box and took all the gold.

Mike took his mom's stuff to Arkell. Arkell said that was a good start, but what Mike was talking about took a lot of gold. Mike offered Arkell money, but Arkell only took gold, so Mike went to another jeweller's in the mall, maxed out his credit card buying gold and took that to Arkell. Arkell said he could do it for twice that.

Mike broke into a jewellery store a few nights later. He got away clean, but it was in all the papers and Arkell must have known, but Arkell took Mike's gold anyway.

Arkell strapped Mike for twelve hours into a chair in the back that looked like a dentist's chair, but afterwards all of his memories of Rebecca were gone. Instead, Mike had memories of a grove of trees a half-hour outside the city. He remembered spending hours just sitting there and it had been good.

Mike took to driving out there after work. He went three or four days a week. There was a stump in the middle of the grove. He just sat on it and enjoyed the forest. Sometimes he'd pick up a pizza or a shawarma on the way, and he'd sit in the grove and eat.

Mike liked sitting in the grove. He even went in the winter. He'd wear extra layers to work and be hot all day so that he could sit out longer without getting cold. One day in the spring when Mike got to the grove, there was a woman there. She said she was Rebecca. She said she used to come to this grove all the time and it was beautiful and she'd really missed it when she'd been living back east.

Rebecca was pretty. Mike asked Rebecca out and she said sure and they got serious. After four years together they got married. They got a dog. They talked about having kids and they even tried, but it turned out Rebecca couldn't have kids, which was okay because the whole thing went to shit ten years in and Rebecca left Mike.

Mike rented an apartment downtown, down the hall from Bruce, who used to be his neighbour years ago, before he'd met Rebecca. They got to talking one day waiting for the elevator, and Bruce told Mike how he used to have a cousin. "Arkell. He had this place in the mall," Bruce said. "Yeah, I think I remember that place," Mike said.

Bruce said probably Mike did remember it. He said Arkell had retired and sold off the business to some woman from Toronto, though. The woman had a website, and Mike sent her an email and set up an appointment. Her place was on Queen Street East. It had a nice shiny storefront and a tray of cupcakes at the cash.

Mike gave her a ring and some stuff that Rebecca'd left behind, and the woman asked how long they'd been together. Mike said ten years, and she said that was awhile. She said usually in a case like that she'd recommend doing just the end. "Do you ever see her around?" she said. "No, she moved down south when we split," Mike said.

The woman recommended that Mike have her killed off. "In your memory. Obviously she won't really be dead," she said, but Mike said no. He said he wanted to forget the whole thing. He said he'd done pretty well the last ten years and finding the gold shouldn't be a problem.

There's a bench downtown near where Mike works where he goes and sits at lunch and after work. He's been going there for as long as he can remember. He sits and watches the people go by. Sometimes he has a feeling like it's not the right bench, but the feeling always passes.

The other day a woman came by and sat down on the bench beside Mike. She told Mike that she used to sit there all the time and just watch the people walk by, before she moved down south. She said her name was Rebecca and Mike said he'd always liked that name, and then he asked her if she'd like to go for dinner with him, and she said she would.

Sad Sacks

WE HAD THESE SACKS WHEN I WAS A KID where we threw our sads. We kept them under our beds and when we went out, our parents always brought one along. When we felt sad, we put our feelings in the sacks.

When the sacks were full our parents threw them out with the garbage and they were gone the next morning.

Me and my sister had happy childhoods. I don't remember crying. I don't remember my friends or my sister crying either.

I never thought anything about it until I went out with Sarah. Sarah saw me one day with a sack, and she said what was it. I said it was a sad sack and didn't she have them when she was a kid. I said I knew a lot of adults didn't like to use them, but I still found them helpful sometimes.

Sarah said she didn't have sad sacks when she was a kid. She said she saw a shrink in university who told her to use them, but she didn't think that was honest. She said she didn't like it that I used them.

I loved Sarah and I wanted to be with her, so I gave up using sad sacks and it was okay. There were a couple of times when Sarah and I fought and afterwards I cried, and once I told her she was a bitch for not letting me use a sad sack, but I didn't use one and most of the time I was happy.

I didn't use a sad sack for eight years, until after we had Lucy and I heard Lucy cry. I knew she was sad, and I knew a sad sack would fix it, so I went to the grocery store and bought a half-dozen of them.

Sarah said to get rid of them. She said they weren't coming into her house, but I kept them anyway. I hid them in the luggage in the closet. I used one for Lucy and one for myself. Lucy stopped crying, and I felt happier about things.

Sarah seemed like she was sad most of the time, though. I asked her if she was okay. I said maybe it was post-partum depression and she should see somebody, but she said she was fine. She said sometimes that was life without sad sacks.

It made me sad to think about Sarah like that and I used the sack more, but it didn't fill up, and then I found Sarah in the closet one day emptying the sack out.

I asked her what the hell she was doing, and she said I didn't understand anything. She said what did I think happened to all the sadness that people got rid of, and I said I didn't know.

Sarah said the sadness didn't just disappear. She said people had to dispose of it. She said she knew how it was. She said her father was a sad sack collector. She said he was miserable and depressed and he died at forty-eight, because he was too sad all the time to take care of himself.

Sarah said it wasn't right what happened to her father and everyone else like him. She said why couldn't people handle their own goddamned sadness.

I sat down beside Sarah and I took her in my arms and told her how sorry I was. Then I told her how happy my childhood was and how happy Lucy's could be and how it didn't have to be for her like it was for her father, and then I took all of Sarah's sadness and put it in sacks. It filled up all six sacks there was so much.

When I was done Sarah smiled at me and kissed me and said she'd never felt better.

Unlovable

I READ IN THE PAPER that Graham killed himself. The paper said he left a note, and the note said Graham killed himself because he was unlovable and he couldn't face that anymore. According to Graham's brother, nobody came forward at the funeral to dispute the note.

I went out with Graham for two years less a day. I wasn't the last woman Graham went out with. Graham's brother said he went out with three women after me and one guy. Graham's brother said I was the only one mentioned in the note, though.

I met Graham online. He was an okay guy. I've been out with some real dicks and Graham wasn't one of them.

Graham wasn't bad looking either, and he was pretty smart, which was why I went out with him for two years less a day, even when I wasn't in love with him.

Graham was insecure about love. He said none of his mother, father or brother loved him.

His mom even told him she didn't love him. She told him that before she'd had kids she'd assumed all mothers loved their kids, but obviously that wasn't so. She said that to Graham's face. She even said it wasn't her, because she loved Graham's brother and maybe it was that Graham was unlovable.

Graham said his father told him not to worry about it. Graham's father said that Graham was one hell of a natural ball player and if he worked a bit harder, he could make it to the majors maybe, and then it wouldn't matter if his family loved him, because other people would love him for being a ballplayer.

Graham's brother said of course he didn't love Graham. "But then, I'm a prick," he said, which he was.

Graham told me he still didn't believe he was unlovable. He said his family was pretty fucked up and with seven billion people in the world there had to be somebody who would love him.

` In his note, Graham said it was when we broke up that he first believed he was unlovable.

In two years less a day, I never told Graham that I loved him. The day before our second anniversary, Graham cornered me in the kitchen and asked me straight up if I loved him, and I told him no.

Graham said sure, but that was right now. He said in two years I must have loved him at some point, and I said that I hadn't.

Graham got tears in his eyes. He said he loved me and if I didn't love him he'd set me free, and I left. Graham said in his note that he thought I'd come back to him, but I didn't.

I've had trouble sleeping since I read about Graham. I think about our relationship. I think about all the moments, big and little. I keep coming back to this one time in Graham's car in the freezing rain where we were sitting there waiting for the car to defrost and "Everybody Needs Somebody to Love" came on and he started singing to it.

He was really into it. He was drumming on the dashboard, and after, we made out. I think maybe I loved him in that moment, which means that he wasn't unlovable, and I killed him because I wanted our relationship to be over, so I didn't tell him that I'd loved him then.

Then I think that I didn't really love Graham then, either, that I just pitied him and that that's what I'm doing now and he really was unlovable.

Either way, I feel like Graham got ripped off. Graham's brother said maybe, but you have to bring that sort of thing on yourself, to not even have your mother love you.

Nothing Left to Say

JOE AND RACHEL HAVE NOTHING LEFT TO SAY to each other. They live on the fourteenth floor and nobody ever hears them talk, and people who've known them a long time wonder why they don't get divorced.

Supposedly they used to say a lot to each other. This one woman, who's lived right below them since back in the sixties when they moved in, says they used to talk constantly. She says she could hear them at four in the morning just talking, and now nothing.

There's a lot of talk about Joe and Rachel though, like how back in the seventies Joe was fucking his secretary and he moved out for six months, and like how their second kid, Ollie, isn't even his.

It's true about the secretary, and it's true about Ollie, and it's true that Joe and Rachel never talk. A few years ago, Joe left. He was gone four years, and everybody assumed it was finally over. People said Joe was old, sure, but he was in shape still and he had some money and they figured he'd shacked up with somebody younger.

That's not how it was, though. Joe went off around the world. He went to find something to say to Rachel. He went to markets and to high-end stores in Europe and Asia and Africa and he even asked around with the guys who sell stuff in the alleys at night, but nobody could tell Joe where to find something more to say.

After four years, Joe went home. Joe and Rachel don't have as much money as some people think and he was out of cash.

Joe got home five years ago now and he and Rachel still don't talk to each other. People shake their heads and wonder why they don't just get it over with and divorce, but the truth is they still love each other, even though Joe moved out for six months in the seventies when he was fucking his secretary, and even though their second kid, Ollie isn't even Joe's.

Joe and Rachel still look at each other though, and sometimes they hold hands when they walk, and sometimes they even still fuck. It's just that they've said everything there is to say to each other.

Samson in the Dumpster

THIS GUY CAME INTO THE BARBERSHOP where I got my hair cut. He asked Tony for a trim, because Tony had the chair at the front of the store. Instead of a trim, Tony took it all off, and after the guy wouldn't move and they stuck him in Lorenzo's chair, because Lorenzo's seventy-five and he's sick half the time and the other half the time he doesn't have any customers anyway.

Tony said you should've seen this guy's hair. He said it was down to his ass and it was so nasty Tony had to wash it first and even then it was gross, but the guy said to only take off an inch or so, just to even up the split ends.

Tony said he was going to do it like the guy wanted because it wasn't his job to argue, but then the guy's girlfriend came in and she was gorgeous and she flirted with Tony while he was washing the guy's hair. According to Tony he got the guy back to his chair and that's when she leaned over and whispered in Tony's ear to take it all off. She licked his earlobe and told him there was a hundred bucks in it for him if he took it all off.

Tony got out the scissors first, because he didn't want to make it too obvious by reaching for the razor. Tony said he pulled the hair back and just sawed through it, and the guy's girlfriend leaned over and kissed the guy on the lips and said already it looked so much better. Tony said the guy must've seen all the hair in Tony's hand, but he didn't say anything and there was a hundred dollars in it for Tony, so he kept cutting.

Tony said he noticed when he went for the razor that the guy was slumping. He said he had to hold up the guy's head to finish. When it was done, Tony and the guy's girlfriend tried to get the guy up, but he wouldn't move.

Tony said the girlfriend started freaking out. "He told me once this would happen, but how was I supposed to know?

And you saw his hair. It was fucking nasty. He had to get it cut. It was disgusting," she said.

Tony told her it was probably just shock and he'd be okay in a bit, but the guy still hadn't moved by closing. He even slid out of the chair at one point and Tony had to wedge him in with one of those booster seats they use for little kids.

Eventually Tony called the paramedics, even though the girlfriend said not to because the paramedics would blame her and Tony, and then she ran out without leaving the hundred dollars. Tony said the paramedics showed up and they said the guy wasn't dead. They said they didn't know what was wrong with him, but he wasn't dead and he wasn't sick and he wasn't in shock and then they left.

After a couple of days the hair grew back a little and the guy perked up a bit. He still couldn't move, but he started to talk. Tony told him he'd take him home. "And don't worry about the haircut. It's on the house," Tony said. The guy said fuck that, he wasn't going home. He said he was staying right there in the chair.

The shop owner told Tony the guy could stay and he could sit in Lorenzo's chair, because Lorenzo was two months behind on the rent anyway, but then Tony'd have to pay rent on Lorenzo's chair too.

I went in for a haircut about two weeks after, and the guy was still sitting in Lorenzo's chair. His hair was growing back in and you could see he had a pretty good bald spot. The guy saw me looking at it and said, "That's right. All because of your buddy here. I had plenty of hair before this butcher got at it, and now it won't grow back and I'm fucked. All I can do is sit here and talk. I can't even get up and get a drink of water. I need him to get it for me. I can't even twitch for fuck's sake."

"How many times do I have to tell you not to bother the customers," Tony said and then he told me to sit down.

The guy didn't listen to Tony. I sat down and the guy said, "Don't do it. You're insane if you let this guy cut your hair." He kept it up through the whole haircut. He kept saying it was crooked and he said how I had a lot of grey for a guy my age and a guy with grey shouldn't have one of those stupid little kid haircuts, had I looked in a magazine in the last twenty years.

Every now and then Tony'd tell him to shut up and then he'd tell me to just ignore him. Whenever Tony'd tell him to shut up, the guy'd say, "How much did she offer you?"

Tony leaned in close to me and said, "What can I do? I feel responsible," and the guy said, "Of course you feel responsible. You are responsible. Haven't you ever heard the story of Samson and Delilah?" "If you don't shut up I'm going to shave that head bald again and keep shaving it everyday," Tony said and the guy shut up for a bit.

"He's scaring off my business," Tony said and then he said, "I've got to pay for the rent on his chair now too. You know it's expensive."

Tony left the back crooked, but I tipped him ten bucks anyway. "Really? The guy butchers your hair like that and you leave him a ten dollar tip?" the guy said.

When I went for my next haircut the guy was still sitting in Lorenzo's chair. His hair had grown back in quite a bit and Tony said the guy could get up and walk around the store as long as someone helped him.

"He's still got that bald patch," I said and the guy leaned over and spat at me. One of the other barbers came up to me after my haircut and told me I had to do something. He said I was the only customer Tony had left. He said the guy was hurting everybody's business, but Tony was in big trouble paying rent for two chairs with no money coming in. I asked the other barber why he didn't do something about the guy if it was that bad, and he said it wasn't his responsibility.

I left Tony an extra fifty. Otherwise I didn't do anything, but somebody did because neither Tony nor the guy is in the barbershop anymore. The rumour is that Tony couldn't make the rent and the owner threw him and the guy out. That's what the barber who cut my hair last time said.

I don't know what happened to Tony, but somebody dumped the guy in the dumpster out back. They'd shaved him clean again and chucked him in headfirst. I turned him over and brushed him off and I don't go to that barbershop anymore.

Vera is Based on my First Girlfriend

I WROTE THIS STORY. IT WAS PRETTY GOOD, maybe a bit pithy, but really interesting characters and an ending that caught you off guard that was happy without being cheesy. I'd say it was one of my better stories. The only problem with the story was that it spoke for itself.

I've always spoken for my stories before. That way the story is how I want it, and when I say that the death of Graham Ericsson signifies the death of liberty, or that Vera is based on my first girlfriend, or that the name of the bar where they meet really doesn't mean shit – I just tried to think of a good name for a bar – there's no one to contradict me.

This story though, has an entirely different interpretation of itself than I do. I don't know why this story speaks for itself. I can't think of what I did when I was writing it that was different from what I normally do. I also can't figure out where this story gets its ideas. Its interpretation of itself is completely flawed. It sees meaning in all these little details where there isn't any, and it clearly doesn't understand its ending.

I sat down with my story and tried to get it to see things my way, but it wouldn't. Worse, it went around telling other people how I didn't even understand my own story. I told it that it was my story, and in future, I just wouldn't read it, but then it crashed a book signing, going around to everyone and telling them that if I couldn't figure out one story that I'd written, probably I was misrepresenting others of my stories too, and then those stories were worthless.

I told my story that I could wipe it out. I pointed out that it hadn't appeared in print anywhere yet, that I'd just read it a couple of places, so all I needed was a match or a paper shredder and a delete button and that would be the end of it.

Two days later I caught my story on CBC's *All in a Day*. It said how I not only didn't understand my own stories, I was trying to suppress them. It said that a story should speak for itself. It said that was its whole message and it was woefully ironic that its author, having written a story about how stories need to speak for themselves, was now threatening to silence it.

It was never about stories speaking for themselves, though, which is why I felt okay after I'd killed it. I mean I did my best by it. I tried to correct it, and when it didn't get it, I warned it, and then when it didn't listen, I followed through.

A few wags have lamented the loss of a great story. A one of a kind that really spoke for itself, the Toronto Review of Books said, but when a story won't listen to reason, what can you do except create an example for future stories.

The Soul of a Poet

I HAVE THE SOUL OF A POET. I bought it at a Sotheby's auction. I can't remember the poet's name. She isn't exactly well known, but I couldn't afford a really famous poet. I don't get poetry anyway. Maybe she's really great and she will be famous one day, although I don't think so.

I keep her soul in a glass case in my sitting room. It's just a mist that swirls around. My friend Meredith looked at it and said I got suckered, but I've got all the certificates of authenticity, and plus I got it from Sotheby's.

Everyone else knows what it is. People come over and they all say how wonderful the house is, and they say I have the soul of a poet. I always wanted to hear that. My grandmother told me once that I had the soul of a banker, but I didn't think I did, and when I went through my stuff, I couldn't find it anywhere. I asked my mom, and she said I didn't have the soul of a banker, or any other soul for that matter. Other people have told me I'm soulless. I never liked to hear that, and now I don't, because I have the soul of a poet.

I created a sealed room where I can let the soul out and be with it. The soul is moody. I had to remove all the breakables from the room, which you wouldn't think would be a problem without a body, but it is.

Sometimes if the soul is in the right mood, she'll speak in verse. It all seems pretty trite to me, a lot of stuff about alcohol and sex and suicide, but I write it down and then when people come over I read it to them. Most people roll their eyes at the verses, but they always listen, and after, they smile at me and they tell me I have the soul of a poet, and that they wished they did too, even if she wasn't any good.

The Greatest Love Of All Time

THE GREATEST LOVE OF ALL TIME was between a Catholic guy and a Jewish woman. It started in the nineteen-thirties in Poland when they were teenagers.

The lovers were split up by World War II. They both wound up in concentration camps, but they both survived. He escaped to Russia and joined the Red Army, because it seemed like the best way to track her down and save her.

His unit liberated her camp at the end of the war, but they didn't see each other. He saw the camp records and the camp records said she was there, but that she'd been gassed, so he didn't look for her.

She wasn't gassed, though. She told a friend about her love and the friend was so moved she took her place. Two days later the camp was liberated.

She went to New York and became an artist. She struggled to get by for a long time. She lived in a tiny studio for thirty years until a gallery on the Upper-West Side did a show of her work, and then she bought a place in Greenwich Village because she was doing okay.

After the war, he was labelled a dissident. He spent twelve years at hard labour and then they gave him a job on an assembly line.

Neither of them married. They got by on their love for each other. He even decided that she couldn't be dead after all and that he'd find her. Even when they masturbated or fucked, they thought about each other.

They met again in 2012 at a restaurant in Mexico City. They recognized each other, and she got up and went over to his table. She fell into his arms and they wept and it was beautiful and it was glorious.

They went to a park and fucked under a tree like teenagers and then they went back to her hotel and fucked again and then they fell asleep in each other's arms.

In the morning he was dead and she was heartbroken. She went downstairs to go for a swim, but she didn't swim. She just sank into the pool and drowned before anyone noticed.

Some sap decided the whole thing was unfair, and he hit the god-damned reset button, which he wasn't authorized to do. How could he not, with a love like that, he said.

After the reset, the couple left Poland for the UK nine months before the blitzkrieg. His father knew some people who got him a job at an IBM plant in Manchester.

The greatest love of all time got through the war just fine. They got married and had three kids. He got homesick. He said he wanted to go back to Poland, and she said no fucking way.

They stopped having sex. They didn't even talk much, but they stayed together awhile for the kids. They split up in 1966. It was really bitter. He moved back to Poland, and she wouldn't let the kids go to see him.

They met again in a restaurant in 2012 in Mexico City. They had dinner together, and she told him she'd remarried to a British guy and the British guy wasn't an asshole like he was. She said it took her a long time to get her life in order after him, and then she said she wished they'd never met in the first place.

He said fuck her. He said she wouldn't have gotten out of Poland if it wasn't for his father who knew somebody at IBM, and if she'd stayed in Poland she probably wouldn't even be alive.

After dinner, he followed her back to her hotel room. He strangled her with a bed sheet and then he ran for it. He slipped on the back stairs and cracked his head open and nobody noticed until later when he was already dead.

The idiot who was responsible for it all says he can't figure out what happened. The idiot who was responsible for it all shifted the blame onto his boss and got his boss fired and then got his boss' job. So now I work for the idiot who was responsible for it all, the idiot who fucked up the greatest love of all time.

Ahmed Blows Up

AHMED BLEW UP. So did a ninety-three Citroen and two Israeli soldiers. After Ahmed blew up he was sent to a halfway house on an old Georgian era estate in the countryside.

The halfway house is huge, which is good, because there are quite a lot of people there. They're all martyrs, the people in the halfway house. There's nobody running the estate that anyone can see, and nobody ever leaves the grounds. Most of them don't even go outdoors.

Most of the martyrs are men, but there are a couple of women. Ahmed shares a room with four other men, a Coptic, a Kamikaze, a Bogomil and another Palestinian, from Ramallah.

It turns out that Ahmed used to go with the other Palestinian's cousin. It was after she dumped him, which was after he lost his job, that Ahmed blew up the checkpoint. Ahmed felt bad about leaving his mom and his sister and his nephew, but Ahmed had a higher calling.

At the halfway house, Ahmed spends most of his days reading the newspapers in the kitchen and waiting to get on the one computer in the halfway house, which is in an alcove at the top of the stairs and is twenty years out of date.

That's how everyone at the halfway house spends their days, except for the crazy French girl. They look to see if they're being talked about.

There's never anything about most of them. There were a couple of articles about Ahmed the day after he blew up, but they just said "another suicide bomber". They didn't even mention his name.

Ahmed asked the other Palestinian guy, whose name is Yasser, if this was all there was. Yasser laughed and said what did he expect, paradise and seventy-two virgins? Ahmed said no, but he'd hoped maybe his dying would make a difference, that maybe his charred body would be the one that finally caused things to change.

Ahmed said, still, one virgin would be nice, and what was the crazy French girl's story, and was her hymen intact?

The crazy French girl is actually Joan of Arc, and she didn't make a difference either really, but she's the only one at the halfway house who doesn't spend her time looking through media reports to see if people are talking about her, because she knows that people are talking about her, even though she's been dead over five hundred years. Joan of Arc's got that over everyone else, because they've all been completely forgotten, which is especially hard for the Bogomil, because he died nine hundred years ago and he's been looking desperately for a mention of himself ever since.

While everyone else is looking through newspapers and waiting to get on the computer, Joan of Arc goes outside and walks around the grounds. When she does this, the guys who are waiting to get on the computer stare out the windows and they muse about whether or not Joan of Arc's hymen is still intact after over five hundred years, but none of them ever dares to approach her, because she's Joan of Arc, and who in hell are they?

Griffs' New Client

WHEN THINGS WERE GOING BADLY FOR JIMMY, he'd put his head in his hands and say he needed something, and something appeared in a day or two.

That was how Jimmy lived. He was always one bad turn away from being in real trouble, and then the bad turn would come and he'd be scared and he'd feel like he couldn't take it anymore. He'd wake up in the middle of the night, usually around four, and he'd go sit on the toilet with his eyes closed and his head in his hands and say he needed something.

It was after one of those nights that Jimmy'd gotten his last job, and the job before that. It was after one of those nights that Jimmy'd won five thousand dollars on the lottery.

Jimmy met Chandra after one of those nights. When he met Chandra he hadn't had a date in three years. He woke up at four in the morning feeling lonely, and he went and sat on the toilet and put his head in his hands and said, "Please let me meet a woman." He met Chandra that afternoon and they were together for four years. Right until the end.

Five months before the end, Jimmy lost his job. He went out and looked for a new job, but he couldn't find anything. By the end, he was broke and all his credit cards were maxed out.

Chandra had a job, but it barely covered the bills and Jimmy owed money and people were calling him at dinnertime to remind him. Jimmy woke up most mornings and went and sat on the toilet and put his head in his hands, but he didn't say anything for five months.

Three days before he died, Jimmy finally said something. He was tired of being broke and scared, but he was also tired of bouncing from one bit of luck to the next. None of the little things was enough and he didn't want to do it anymore. Three days before he died, Jimmy put his head in his hands and said, "I need something big."

Two days went by and nothing big happened. Jimmy figured that something big would take longer to pull together than just something, so he didn't really sweat it.

At two-thirty-three in the afternoon on the third day, Jimmy got hit by a bus on the Mackenzie King Bridge. Jimmy saw the bus when it smacked into him and realized that it was something big. It wasn't what Jimmy'd had in mind, but he figured god knew what he was doing.

God had no idea about any of it. Jimmy lay there on the bridge and so did his soul. It didn't take off to a better place. It just lay there on the Mackenzie King Bridge flattened, like Jimmy. Meanwhile, the bus driver ran around and around the bus going, "fuck, oh fuck," because he was fucked.

The driver was sure he was going to lose his job for having a dead guy under his bus. And if any of the passengers at the front squealed about how he was texting, or somebody at the company checked his cell phone records, he might even face jail time.

God wasn't responsible for any of this, though. It was a gnome with a white beard who refused to wear a hat. The gnome was named Griffs. Griffs was responsible for everything. He'd even sent the text message that the driver was reading when the bus hit Jimmy.

Griffs ran a service. He'd taken on Jimmy as a client on a referral from Jimmy's ex-girlfriend. Griffs had just been starting out then. Now he had a few clients, and they all paid better than Jimmy.

Griffs had been looking for one good, high-paying client for a while, but he wasn't sure he wanted the extra work. He was already doing okay for himself. He had a walk up in Greenwich Village, but New York got cold in the winter and he'd had it in mind to buy a place down south for the winters, maybe in Mexico.

Jimmy was Griffs' only Canadian client. Jimmy lived in Ottawa and Griffs didn't like Ottawa because there was never anything going on, and because the winters were even colder than in New York.

Jimmy was never specific about what he wanted. Some of Griffs' clients really spelled it out, like Griffs was a monkey's paw or something, but Jimmy always just said "I need something."

"Something big" seemed like a good opportunity for Griffs. Griffs figured getting rid of Jimmy could even improve his reputation. People thought you were better at a job like that if you were a little bit crazy.

Griffs had a new client in less than a week. She was a high-powered corporate executive from Shanghai. The contract was worth a hundred times what Jimmy's was worth.

With the extra money Griffs bought a place in Monte Carlo, although he still prefers to spend most of his time in New York.

Heartless

I HAD MY HEART STOLEN. It was careless, but he seemed trustworthy and he was really good looking.

His name was Miguel. He was from Barcelona and he was doing his Masters he said, and he bought me a coffee and we wound up back at my place. My roommate, Claire, said what was I doing with some guy from Barcelona who was only here for eight months. I said it wasn't a big deal. I said I knew he'd be going back and it would all be over and I was okay with that.

Miguel was suave. He wasn't some butcher who'd steal your heart after one night in the sack. We were together for four months. We hung out in cafés and on patios, and at night we'd go to his place or mine and fuck. Miguel was good at fucking.

The last night, we were at my place. Claire was out. We fucked like we always did and then I fell asleep in his arms. When I woke up in the morning, Miguel was gone and there was a fresh incision in my chest.

I stumbled down the hallway to Claire's room. I opened the door and staggered in and collapsed on top of Claire on her bed.

Claire said what the hell? She said she didn't get in until four in the morning. I said I was sorry. I said I thought Miguel had stolen my heart and I needed her help.

Claire sat up in bed. She said let her see, so I showed her. I said we needed to find Miguel and get my heart back, and Claire said it was too late for that.

Claire knew a thing or two about it. She had an ex-boyfriend who used to work for a guy. She said Miguel had to be a pro, because the incision was too clean, and a pro wouldn't hang onto the heart. She said probably he had a buyer and he'd already moved it, but she'd call her ex and ask him to see what he could find out.

Claire's ex called around. He got back to us and said there was a store on College that had just gotten in a young female heart. He said he knew the guy who ran the store and he'd told the guy to hold onto the heart until Claire and I showed up. Claire's ex said the guy owed him a favour.

When we showed up at the store, my heart was gone. The guy who ran the store had a fat face and scraggly facial hair. He said could he see the incision, so I showed him. He said I was lucky. He said that was the work of a pro and it could've been a lot worse. Then he said he was sorry, but he didn't have the heart anymore. He said he'd had one hell of an offer, and how was he to know if the heart was really mine anyway.

Claire called the guy a fucking asshole. She said when her ex told him we were coming, he should've held onto the heart.

The guy said look, he wasn't running a charity, and Claire's ex had said we were students and we didn't have any money and he'd shelled out ten grand for my heart, if it was my heart.

Claire said fine, he'd sold it, who'd he sell it to. The guy said just somebody who'd walked in off the street.

Claire said that was bullshit. She said if he'd bought it for ten, for sure he'd sold it for twenty and what were the odds somebody'd just walked in off the street with twenty grand in their pocket.

The guy shrugged and said he didn't really care what we thought, but Claire said the police might, and the guy gave us an address in Rosedale. He said the guy he'd sold it to was named Harry.

We went to Harry's place. Harry's place was a mansion, and the fucker lived alone. When Harry came to the door and Claire told him about the heart, he said that was a shame, but he didn't have it.

Claire said, okay, sorry to bother you, and then she kicked my feet out from under me and I went splat onto Harry's patio stones. My chest really hurt and I couldn't get up. Harry bent down to see if I was all right and Claire ducked past him and went inside.

Harry left me and went after Claire. He left the door open and I could hear them. Claire said what the hell was this, and Harry said it was a cooler, what did it look like. I heard Claire flip it open, and then she said it was a cooler with a human heart in it and wasn't that the coincidence.

Harry said it was a coincidence. He said that heart was a perfect specimen and anyone could see I wasn't in any kind of shape. Claire said of course I wasn't, I'd had my heart ripped out of my chest, but if he looked at my muscle tone, it was clear I took care of myself.

I dragged myself to the doorway and called out that we could prove it with a DNA test. Harry said sure we could, but he wasn't going to pay for it and he was pretty sure we didn't have the money. He said besides, by the time the results came back, the heart wouldn't be good for anything.

Harry said he'd been looking for a specimen like that for a long time and he had to get the lacquering process underway before the heart lost its colour, and as for putting it back in my chest, if it was my heart, time had to be almost up on that.

Claire said let's call the police and see what they said. Harry said fine, but in the meantime, it was his heart and we'd better get the fuck off his property. Claire tried to slip by him and out the door with my heart, but he grabbed her and threw her against the wall and she dropped it. After that, he pushed her out and slammed the door right in our faces.

Claire called the police, and the police said did we have any proof. Claire said it was my heart for Christ's sake, and the officer said he understood, but did we have any proof.

Claire hung up the phone and helped me up. She said she was sorry, and then she called us a cab.

My chest healed pretty well. Miguel knew what he was doing. I don't feel the same way since it happened, though. I've been out with a few guys and a couple of them have fallen for me. I've told them I'm in love too, but I'm not and I hurt them. I never would have done that before.

Miguel came to see me once a few years later. He knocked on my door one evening and I let him in. Miguel said he was sorry for what he'd done. He said he'd been in a tight spot, he'd had some people after him and it was just one of those things. He said he felt terrible about it.

I said sure, I understood. Miguel begged me to forgive him. I told him I did, but I didn't. I remembered what Claire and the guy at the pawnshop said: about how it was the work of a pro. That meant Miguel was a liar too.

I asked Miguel if he wanted some tea, and then I went to the kitchen. I put the kettle on and I grabbed the butcher's knife from the block. I had the knife behind my back when I came out and I took Miguel by surprise.

After I had Miguel's heart, I whipped it off the balcony, turned off the stove and went for a walk.

It wasn't a professional job. The police were stationed all around my building waiting for me when I got back. In court, the prosecutor said I showed no remorse, like I was completely heartless, he said.

Vrnjacka Banja

SOPHIA READ SOMETHING ON THE INTERNET about people who were in love who engraved their names on locks and attached the locks to bridges and then threw away the keys. The idea was to keep their love from being stolen or something.

Sophia and I were in love and we thought we should do it. Some couples in Toronto had attached locks to a bridge on the Humber River, but the city cut the locks and told the lovers to fuck off. Sophia said that wasn't real anyway, attaching a lock to a bridge on the Humber River.

Sophia said she'd read that the whole thing had started in Serbia, in a place called Vrnjacka Banja. Supposedly a local woman lost her boyfriend to a Greek woman during World War I, and she committed suicide and the other local women started to lock up their love to keep that from happening to them.

Sophia had a great grandmother from Serbia and she wanted to go to Vrnjacka Banja and put our lock on the Most Ljubavi. She showed me a picture of the Most Ljubavi. It was a little footbridge in a park surrounded by trees with a little stream underneath it. I said it looked lovely.

We went to Vrnjacka Banja and we put a lock engraved with our initials on the Most Ljubavi. It was May and everything was in bloom, and after we attached the lock we kissed and then we threw the key into the water.

Twelve years later, Sophia left me. I asked her how she could leave me. I said I thought we'd locked up our love together so that it couldn't escape.

Sophia said the lock was a symbol, and it was a symbol of who we were then, not who we were now. She said it was weird, though, because for a long time she'd thought about that lock and she'd felt like it was holding her back from leaving me. Sophia said she'd gotten over that, though.

She said anyway, we were too old to cling to some silliness about locks and bridges, and then she left me and I was devastated.

I didn't believe it, that the lock was just a symbol, so I went back to Vrnjacka Banja to check on our lock. I went to the Most Ljubavi first thing in the morning and looked through the locks until well into the afternoon, and our lock wasn't there.

I asked a park worker about the locks and he shrugged. I went over and I grabbed the park worker by the arm and I said who'd sabotaged the locks? The park worker said in English that he didn't understand English, and I pulled him over to the bridge and pointed at the locks and said who?

The park worker pointed. He said the white building, apartment fourteen, Dmitrios. I went over to the building. The front door wasn't locked and I went in and up the stairs and down to the end of the hallway to apartment fourteen.

I banged on the door and a man said "go away" in English, but with a heavy accent. A woman's voice said why would he say "go away" in English around here?

I banged on the door again and a woman opened it and said what the hell did I want? I said I wanted to talk to Dmitrios. The woman said he was indisposed. The woman was about thirty and she was pretty.

Dmitrios' apartment was a dump. The walls were cracked and it was just one room with a cement floor and a futon against one wall, with a little square TV on a stand in front of it, and a kitchen table and chairs in the corner.

There was a withered old man on the futon. I asked the old man if he was Dmitrios. The woman said never mind who he was. She said I was intruding and the real question was who was I and what did I want? Dmitrios said I wanted the same thing she wanted.

I said really, what did she want? She said to mind my own fucking business. Dmitrios said she wanted the same thing I wanted.

I said I wanted to know why he'd cut off my lock. Dmitrios said he knew that. He said the only person who ever

126

came by who didn't want to know that was his brother's daughter, Branka.

I said so why did he do it? Dmitrios said don't ask him that, because he wouldn't say. I said if he wouldn't say then tell me why I shouldn't just kill him, and Dmitrios shrugged. The woman said, yes, and why should she stop me, and Dmitrios shrugged again and said it would at least put him out of his misery.

The woman said maybe that was why I shouldn't do it, because a bastard like him should suffer, the same way everyone whose locks he cut off suffered.

Dmitrios said they didn't all suffer. He said what about our partners in the locks, were they suffering? The woman said she'd made a pact and Terry had too, and Terry never would have broken that pact, that it was Dmitrios who had broken the pact for him. She said Dmitrios had ruined the best thing that had ever happened to her life.

There was another knock on the door and another woman, fiftyish, in a power suit, came in. The first woman said what did she want, and I said yeah, what did she want, and couldn't she see we were busy? Dmitrios said she wanted the same thing that we wanted, which turned out to be true. The first woman said that was three people in less than an hour, and it was obvious that Dmitrios was a serial lock cutter. She said we should make him suffer.

The second woman agreed and the two of them slapped Dmitrios and spat in his face. They told him to tell them why he'd done it. They said they wouldn't stop until he told them, and the bastard got a hard on.

I went to the kitchen drawers and found a book of matches. I pulled off Dmitrios' socks and shoved the matches between his toes. The first woman sat on his legs to keep him from squirming. Once I'd gotten matches between all of his toes, I lit them.

Dmitrios lost his hard on. He said put out the god damned matches already and he'd talk.

I blew out the matches. Dmitrios said the women could keep slapping him and spitting on him if they wanted to, and

127

they said he was a disgusting pig. He said yeah, that was it, and they said just tell us why he'd cut the locks off.

Dmitrios said fine, if that was what we wanted. He said really, we were amateurs, though. He said twenty years ago, even five years ago, he wouldn't have told us just because we'd lit his feet on fire, but he was getting old.

Dmitrios said he cut the locks to help us. He said he had a lock on the bridge once. He said he and his wife, Anastasija, put it on when they were just teenagers. He said eventually Anastasija got tired of him and she wanted a divorce, but she couldn't tell him, because of the lock.

He said Anastasija got so desperate that she hired a locksmith to undo the lock for her. After the lock was off, Anastasija shacked up with the locksmith. Dmitrios said he went over there when he found out, and they were in bed together.

He said they'd left the lock on the counter in the kitchen and Dmitrios heated it up on the stove until it started to melt and then he poured half of it down the locksmith's throat. Dmitrios said he might not look like it now, but back then he was strong and it was easy for him to force the locksmith. He said he was going to pour the other half down Anastasija's throat, but Anastasija screamed so loudly that the cops came and hauled Dmitrios off before he could.

Dmitrios said he'd been mad with rage. He said he wished he could go back and change it. He said he'd had no one to blame but Anastasija and the locksmith, but it didn't have to be like that for others. He said that's how it would have been for us, that eventually our partners would have come and taken the locks off themselves if it hadn't been for him. He said he'd saved them and us, because he was the one who'd cut off our locks, so now we had him to blame.

We all sat there stunned. While we sat there stunned, a huge guy in a leather jacket burst through the door shouting in an Italian accent about how he was going to kill Dmitrios.

The guy went straight to Dmitrios and picked him up by the throat and strangled him. The two women and I tried to stop him, but we didn't try very hard.

Heaven's Gone to Hell

THE DEVIL GOT THIS IDEA back in the nineteenth century, during the industrial revolution. The idea was to put out the fires of hell.

Water and sand weren't much good in hell. They could clear a little space, but it didn't take long for the fires to overrun it again. The devil figured that new technologies coming out of the industrial revolution could help.

The devil needed bodies for his plan, so he started to recruit firefighters. It took until the early twenty-first century before he was satisfied with his firefighting corps. Then the devil called all the firefighters in at once and told them about his plan.

He said hell had been a nice place back in the day, back before god had decided to damn it by engulfing it in flames. The devil said it wasn't fair to make people spend eternity in that for a couple of minor transgressions. He said he wanted to reclaim hell for all the sinners and he needed their help.

The firefighters weren't so eager to help. The spokesman said it was suddenly clear to him how it was. He accused the devil of duping them all into sinning for his own personal gain. One of the firefighters said she'd heard that heaven had an appeals process, and when god heard about how the devil had seduced them all, god would forgive them.

The devil said what did it matter if they were seduced. He said they'd still sinned, so they were damned, and the firefighters told him to fuck off.

The firefighters tried to appeal to heaven. They got in touch with a guy who used to be a lawyer and knew about this stuff. The lawyer told them to forget it. He said nobody had ever successfully appealed to heaven.

The firefighters tried anyway, but they didn't get anywhere. The main problem was that heaven insisted all appeals be filled out by hand on paper, and the paper burned up instantly in the fires that were everywhere in hell.

The firefighters went back to the devil and said they were willing to listen. They said what did the devil have in mind?

The devil said there were a few top-notch chemists in hell who had come up with an agent for putting out the fires. The devil said all he needed now was a crack troop of firefighters. He said if they put out the fires and still wanted to leave, he'd even support their applications.

The firefighters said they weren't taking that chance, but they'd help for a share of whatever the devil got out of the venture.

The devil said okay, and the firefighters got to work. It took two and a half years, but the firefighters put out all the fires except for a couple of small, subterranean ones that just started up again as soon as the firefighters turned their backs.

The firefighters had to stay on the couple of subterranean fires all the time, but there were more than enough of them for the work, so that each one only had to put in twelve hours every other week, which is pretty good for hell.

With the fires out, it looked like the devil had end played god. All the ash from the fires made the soil in hell really fertile, and there were some beautiful beaches with water that you could swim in year round.

With the fires out, hell was actually a nicer destination than heaven, and people took to a life of sinning in order to get in. God tried to counter by claiming that a life of virtue was its own reward, but people tuned him out.

God switched tacks and said that heaven was safe because it was filled with the best souls, while hell was full of depraved maniacs, but a Stanford study showed that people would rather the adventure of an afterlife filled with depraved maniacs than the boredom of a bunch of church going goodie-goodies.

It seemed for sure like the devil had won, but then god declared a general amnesty and everyone from hell was relocated to heaven. Now there's nobody left in hell except the devil and he can't keep the fires from starting up again by himself.

So god's won, but the people who know say that heaven's gone to hell since the amnesty.

Saints and Sinners

WE HAD THIS GAME WHEN I WAS A KID, Saints and Sinners. It was one of those games with a spinner that told you what to do. The board had trees and mountains and deserts and oceans and fields and marshes, and the trees and mountains stuck out of the board.

At the start of the game, you had to decide whether you wanted to be a saint or a sinner, and then you took the appropriate path. If you were a saint, you had to climb this really high mountain in the middle of the mountains, surrounded by desert and you had to do it with a sick stranger on your back.

If you were a sinner, you had to make your way to a chasm in the middle of the ocean.

The game was easier if you were a sinner. Some of the rules didn't apply to sinners and the chasm in the ocean was three spaces closer to the start than the mountain and it was easier to get to, because you could take a boat.

The rules for the game claimed that it was true to life. They said that sinning was easier at first, but harder at the end. The point was to show you how sinning was a spiral. At the start, the sinner had to steal a chocolate bar. Later on the sinner had to fuck his neighbour's wife. At the end, after the sinner steals the boat, and before he dives into the abyss, he has to drown his best friend.

Drowning your best friend is supposed to be too horrible even to contemplate, but I never had any trouble with it. I played the game a lot, and the sinners almost always won.

My mom didn't like that I always played a sinner. My dad said it was just a game, and my mom said she didn't like the game. My dad said she was making too big a deal out of it. He said the game was teaching life lessons.

When I played with friends, they were sometimes sinners too, but my parents and my little brother Joey were always saints. I could tell sometimes my dad wanted to be a sinner, but my mom wouldn't let him. I whipped my family when we played.

Later on, I tested to see whether or not the game really was true to life. I started like in the game, by stealing a chocolate bar. Stealing the chocolate bar went fine, so I kept sinning.

I did well with life, way better than my parents or Joey.

I played life through to the end and I smoked it. I made millions. I had a yacht and a wife and girlfriends and kids and when I got to the part where I took Joey out on my yacht to drown him in the abyss that was okay too.

You'd think at the end I'd be damned, but you'd be wrong. They gave me the third degree at the gate. They tried to claim that my passport was a fake, but I didn't give in and eventually they got god involved.

God came down and looked at me and said my papers were good. He said he'd approved them personally.

I found out later that Joey didn't get in. He'd been planning a trek to the mountains, but I drowned him before he could set out. God said he didn't need some noble failure. God said there was a holy war coming dammit, and sometimes in a holy war, you had to do things you wouldn't normally do.

God said welcome, by the way. He said to take a month and just enjoy heaven, and then we'd get down to it. He said he was looking forward to working with me.

Completing Angie

ANGIE WAS SIX YEARS OLDER THAN ME and she was hot, but she went out with me anyway. Jerry, who introduced us, told me not to go out with her. He said there was something wrong with her. He said he didn't know what, but he'd heard from a couple of guys who'd gone out with her, and it was bad. I didn't listen to Jerry, because Jerry was an idiot.

I went out to dinner with Angie. We went to a really nice place downtown, and after, we went for a walk along the canal, and at the end she let me kiss her goodnight.

We went for dinner again, at a little hole in the wall on Wellington and we split dessert, and after, we went for a walk again, and then we made out and it all seemed pretty normal.

I really liked Angie. She'd thought a lot about a lot of stuff and I loved talking to her. She never said anything about how I was six years younger than her or anything, either.

The only thing that was kind of weird was that it took us a long time to have sex, and when we did have sex, she wouldn't take her clothes off. I said it was awkward to fuck with our clothes on, especially hers, and she said she was sorry. She said it was a fetish and she couldn't explain it.

It wasn't just about sex, though. She always locked the door when she went to the bathroom, even if it was just to shower and she always came out fully dressed.

I did my best not to think about it. I tried to convince myself it didn't matter. Angie was really hot in her clothes and everybody had a fetish, and everything else was great.

One night me and Angie went cross-country skiing along the river and she stopped in the middle of the trail and took off her skis and we were all alone and she knelt down in front of me and asked me to marry her.

I thought about it for a second and then I told her I would, but only if she'd let me see her naked. I said just once. I said after that we could have sex with our clothes on for the rest of our lives, but I had to see her naked the one time.

Angie said okay, and after skiing we went back to her place and had some cider, and then we went up to her bedroom and she stripped naked. Mostly Angie had a really nice body, but there was a section of her stomach on the right side that wasn't there.

The missing section was a weird shape, like a piece from a jigsaw puzzle, and it didn't ooze or anything and it wasn't red. It was like a really old scar or something, except that there wasn't any scar tissue. There wasn't even any skin.

I figured somebody must've done something to her. Probably she'd been really young. I wondered if it had been an accident. I reached out my hand to touch it and she said no.

She went to the top drawer of her dresser. She pulled out something wrapped in cellophane and gave it to me. She said it was her. She said she'd never been complete before, but with me she finally felt like she could be.

I tried to complete Angie. I unwrapped the cellophane and took the piece of her. It was the same shape as the hole in her stomach. I turned the piece around until it lined up and then I tried to put it in. My hand slipped a bit and the piece wasn't quite right and I had to adjust it. The piece felt weird. I expected it to feel like cardboard, but it was soft and fleshy.

I got the piece lined up properly and I pushed it, but it wouldn't go. Angie said do what I had to. She said not to be afraid of hurting her. I pushed harder, but it still wouldn't go. Angie lay down on the bed and I knelt over top of her and pushed as hard as I could and a whole bunch of pieces popped out of her, including parts of her organs.

Angie gasped and I grabbed her shoulders and told her I loved her so much and I told her she'd be okay, even though I didn't believe it.

I ran to the kitchen and grabbed the roll of cellophane and wrapped all the pieces individually. Then I got Angie dressed and drove her to the hospital.

At the hospital, they asked who I was, and I said the fiancé. I tried to explain what had happened and how desperate it was, and they told us to wait. We had to wait four hours to see a doctor and Angie kept getting paler.

The doctor let me stay in the room while he examined Angie. He shook his head and said he'd never seen anything like it. Then he said to give him the pieces. He unwrapped them one by one and fit them in. He pushed them gently into place with his fingertips. The last piece he put in was the one Angie'd given to me. He fit it in no problem and then he discharged her.

I drove Angie home and I stayed the night. In the morning I broke it off with her. She begged me not to. She said why would I do that, when just last night I'd told her how much I loved her. Then she said I was making too much of it. She said he was a doctor and that's what doctors do. She said it wasn't a big deal, but we both knew it was.

My High School Art Teacher Said I Had Talent

THIS WOMAN CAME IN AND SAT DOWN and said she'd always wanted to be an artist. She said she'd quit her job so she could do it, but most of the time she stared at the canvas and when she did paint or sketch something it was always shit.

I told her we didn't take shit artists, and she said she'd read all about us and she had the money and she'd brought her portfolio and her high school art teacher'd said she had talent.

"That's not my department," I said. I took her portfolio out to Dominic and came back. "My job is to find out why you want to be here and to determine whether or not you can handle it," I said.

She said she wanted to be here because of all the endorsements by great artists. She said it was dizzying how many of them swore by us. I told her that was different, because they came to us for a reminder of how it used to be. I told her we weren't a substitute. "Give the money to charity or something and go live on the street," I said.

She said she would, but she was married and her husband made good money and it wasn't fair to ask him to quit his job and suffer with her. I said leave him then, and she said she loved him and she couldn't do that, not ever.

"That makes it hard," I said. "You know people don't come out of here okay," I said, and she said wasn't that the point. Then she said that the website said all these great artists kept coming back.

I said that was true, but they were mostly batshit. Then I asked her some questions about the rest of her life: kids, parents, dogs, cats, where she lived, that sort of thing. After a bit Dominic came in with her portfolio and handed it to me. They just put an eight and a half by eleven at the front of the portfolio. They stamp it with pass or fail. She passed, but I had the final say.

I told her I was sorry, but she didn't have it. She said that couldn't be. "My high school art teacher said I had talent. My husband says I have talent. Even my mom says I have talent and she's a real bitch most of the time," she said.

I shrugged and said sorry, and she said could she at least see what the evaluator wrote. I gave her back her portfolio and told her to go home. She opened up the portfolio and saw the paper and said what the fuck. "It says pass," she said.

I said yeah, but that was only one part of the evaluation. She asked me if it was because she was a woman and I thought she couldn't take it. I said it wasn't, but really it was. She said she'd give me a blow job if it would help. She said hell, she'd even fuck me if that was what it took to prove how serious she was. As long as I didn't tell her husband, she said.

I told Dominic how I'd done it and how I was an asshole who needed help. Dominic said not to be so hard on myself. "She was cute man. Besides, the whole point is to torture them," he said and then he laughed.

When I took the job, they made me sit in on a couple of sessions, so I'd know the kind of stuff they did. "That way you won't be tempted to let somebody in who can't hack it," they said. Dominic was only responsible for judging their ability, so they didn't make him sit in.

They tortured the shit out of this woman. They torture the shit out of everybody. Some of the great ones seem to like it. The famous ones, once they've been, they don't need to go through the review process again. I told Dominic that the woman wouldn't be able to take it and I shouldn't have let her in. He said whatever, it happened and I got laid, right. He said what about that writer who hadn't written a word in over forty years who came in every other week and even knew the torturers by name.

"Have another beer. Besides, maybe you'll be wrong. Maybe she'll be a great artist and you can tell everyone how you fucked her," Dominic said. "She certainly had talent," he said.

I didn't do her outtake. Lisa did it. Lisa said the woman was pretty seriously messed up. She said she went on about how I'd fucked her, and then she started throwing stuff and asking where I was because she was going to kill me.

A week after the woman left, she threw a cast iron frying pan at her husband's head and then she walked out on him. She died on the street nine months later. The police said she'd od'd.

A couple of people on the street who knew her said she carried around a canvas everywhere. They said she told them she'd done it herself. The cop who'd found her said he hadn't seen it, but it turned up in his house.

The police gave it to her husband, who put it up for auction, with the proceeds to go to Amnesty International to fight against torture. The canvas sold for seventeen point one million. Everyone agrees it's absolutely brilliant.

Now there's a copy of the painting on the website, right at the top before any of the testimonials or anything. Dominic showed me. He slapped me on the back and said, see I'd fucked one of the greatest artists of our generation. That afternoon, I walked into my boss's office and quit.

Swimming Lessons At Three

I ANSWERED AN AD IN THE PAPER a week after we defaulted on the rent. Patty bugged me about the rent and about not having a job the whole week. She called me a bum. "How hard is it to get a job?" she said. I said it wasn't that hard, but the jobs were all shit.

"So what? The deal was you'd work, remember? I'm working my ass off at school and my creepy thesis supervisor keeps suggesting dinner at his place, all so we can have a better life. All you have to do is check your brain and go do some job five days a week and you can't even do that."

The ad said you could make upwards of ten grand a week. It said there was travel, medical and dental and flexible hours. I figured it had to be some sort of pyramid scheme, but I answered the ad anyway because I needed money for rent before the landlord kicked us out.

When I called a guy answered. He said his name was Joe. Joe said he'd had lots of calls, but I should come see him anyway so I did. We met downtown and Joe bought me a coffee.

"It's repossession work. Well, it's sort of repossession anyway. It's shit work so nobody wants it, but it's got a lot of perks. Lots of travel for one thing. Overseas. Paris, London, Rome, Tokyo, Beijing, all over really, and all paid for," Joe said.

The job was to collect kids. Not kidnapping or murder or anything, just making sure that the kids who were supposed to go did. Mostly it was accidents or illnesses. Joe said the position had been vacant a year and a half, since he'd fired the last collector.

"She got all guilty feeling about it and she started faking deaths. She'd plant stories in newspapers, that kind of thing. When I got suspicious, she had a couple of families fake funerals. She worked a hell of a lot harder making these kids look dead than she would've had to to kill them. With all that, it's been two years since a kid anywhere has died," he said.

I asked Joe if he had anything else, seniors, even the middle-aged, but he said no. "It's easy to find somebody to repossess the adults. Lots of otherwise functional people have mommy and daddy issues. That's why this is so tricky. I can't just grab some psycho off the street. I need somebody professional."

I told him I understood, but I couldn't do it, and he said that was okay. Then the landlord went to the landlord tribunal to get us evicted, and I called Joe back. Joe said nobody had taken the position yet. He said it was my lucky day. He said he came close to hiring another guy, but he wanted me. He said the moment he saw me he knew I was his guy.

He gave me two to start, both local. "I know how it is. You need to get back on your feet, so a couple of simple ones to start." The first one was a drowning. The second one was a car accident. I took care of both. I had to set it up and watch and take pictures and then go to the funerals to make sure. It was shitty work and I almost quit, but then Joe handed me four thousand cash for maybe twelve hours work.

I gave the landlord his rent in cash and I got some flowers and a nice bottle of wine. I told Patty about the job at dinner. "The pay's incredible. I've already made four grand. Oh and they want me to go to Paris next week. They said they'd pay for you too if you want to go," I said.

Patty asked what the hell kind of job I could get that would pay like that. I told her and she said I was sick. "How could you even think about doing a job like that? Jesus," she said. Then she said if I didn't quit she'd leave me.

"Hey, you were the one who insisted I get a job," I said and she said, "Yeah, but a normal job. How do you even get a job like that?" I said you answered an ad in the paper, and then I said I wouldn't quit.

Patty left me like she said she would. She shacked up with her thesis supervisor. Her friend Amanda said what did I expect, they'd been fucking for months.

I kept working for Joe. Usually it wasn't so bad. I'd go some place and work for a couple of hours and then I'd go and see the sights. It was lonely though, and sometimes it got me down, especially after, watching the families.

Joe arranged parties and retreats and shit for other people who did the same work. I hated the parties because the other people didn't like me. I was the only one who did kids and they all thought that was sick. I made twice what they did, though.

I talked to Joe about it a few times, and he said not to think about it. "I'm paying you a shit load of money. When it gets too bad, go find a whore," he said. I took his advice and it helped.

One time when I was feeling especially bad, Joe pointed out how much the department had shrunk. "Look at it this way, at the turn of the last century there were thirty-four hundred people doing your job and sometimes they had trouble keeping up with the volume. Now it's just you and you've got all sorts of spare time."

I did it for fifteen years and then one day Joe gave me a file on a kid out in Victoria. The file listed the parents and Patty was the mother. I called her at two in the morning, which was only eleven there.

She heard my voice and asked me what I wanted. I told her I just wanted to reconnect. I asked her what she was doing, and she said she was a professor. "I married my supervisor. We've got a boy who's going to be seven in a couple of weeks. How are you? You're not still doing that job are you?" she said.

I told her I was and she said, "You're not calling about Jacob are you?"

"Yeah, but I won't do it Patty. I've got lots of cash saved up. I don't ever need to work again. I'll just tell him I quit," I said. She hung up, but she called me back a couple of hours later. "I want you to do it. If it's going to happen, I'd rather it was someone I knew," she said.

I told her no. "After the last person got fired there was nobody for a year and a half. They had to cancel a whole bunch of planned repossessions. Even if they don't cancel it, that's still a year and a half," I said.

"They could hire somebody next week," she said, and then she repeated that she wanted me to do it. "I don't want to see you, though," she said.

I went out to Victoria and set the whole thing up like I was supposed to. Patty picked the kid up from swimming lessons at three. At ten after she ran a red light and her car got hit by an oncoming SUV. The car flipped over and caught on fire.

I ran over to the car and yanked Patty out of it, and this guy came up to me and started yelling about his commission. I recognized him from one of Joe's parties. I told him to fuck off and then I punched him, right there in front of all the bystanders.

The guy got fired for making a scene. He didn't get his commission either, because Patty lived. Joe lectured me for an hour and a half and then he sighed and said, "Maybe it's the stress. Take a couple of weeks. Then, if you want, there's a vacancy in the adult collections branch."

I took the two weeks and then I went back to work. I still do kids. The pay's good and I'm used to it. If I quit, somebody else will have to get used to it.

Bottled Happiness

WE ALL MADE FUN OF JOEY because Joey was small and he was a spaz and he was kind of a shit.

Joey never said anything when we made fun of him and he didn't try to get even. Not even the time Tyler and Eric tied Joey's hands behind his back and threw him in the river, and he might have drowned except some couple came along and pulled him out and gave him mouth to mouth.

The couple asked Joey what had happened, but Joey didn't tell. They said it was important, that people couldn't do stuff like that, and Joey didn't tell. The couple thought maybe Joey's dad was responsible and they called Children's Aid, and Children's Aid came to the house and then the police came to the house, and Joey still wouldn't tell.

It didn't make us respect Joey, though. We just thought he was an idiot, and we kept on making fun of him. Tyler and Eric threatened to kill Joey if he told about the river, and Joey didn't say anything. He didn't say how he'd kept his mouth shut even when the police came. He just stood there while Tyler and Eric punched his arm.

When we got to high school people started to talk about Joey. They said he'd bottled a lot up for a long time and one day he'd burst, but we still didn't stop. Shun said he didn't understand how somebody could have no friends, and Marcie said Joey must have friends and then she made up a bunch for him.

We gave Joey's fake friends birthdays and hobbies and we left notes in his locker from them. We left a note from his fake girlfriend about how she couldn't believe how small his cock was and she'd never seen one that small and she couldn't even grab it right it was so small.

Tanya said be careful. She said a guy as quiet as Joey was going to kill somebody someday. She said it should be Tyler or

Eric, but probably it would be some poor sap on the street who asked Joey what time it was or something. Shun said he didn't think so. He said Joey was too much of a wimp to kill someone else, and he'd end up by killing himself instead.

Joey didn't kill himself, or anyone else either. He went into business. He sold the emotions he'd bottled up over the years. He sold it to a few athletes, and the athletes all had their best performances and suddenly Joey was swamped with demand.

Joey put an ad on the internet for losers and jilted lovers and anyone who was pissed or bitter or resentful. He bought their emotions, bottled them and sold them for a big mark up.

There was a fight one night at a tennis match between two guys who'd drunk bottles of rage beforehand. The one guy got killed from a graphite splinter that went through his windpipe. There was an inquiry and the government decided it wasn't such a good idea to sell anger and bitterness and resentment, and they banned it.

Joey didn't skip a beat. He switched to selling happiness, which sold way better than rage ever did. Joey hired people who were happy and bottled that. To keep people happy he gave them drugs and junk food and porn and told them how valuable they were to him.

Joey hired on Tyler and Eric and me and a whole bunch of others who used to make fun of him. Business was good, so Joey bought the old coke bottling plant in the west end and reopened it. Joey sells happiness and hope and love and people lap it up.

Joey's rich now. It's hard sometimes working for Joey. It's exhausting being happy all day, and after my shift I feel drained. Joey pays us pretty well, though, so at the end of the day I grab a bottle of happiness and it perks me right up, and nobody makes fun of Joey anymore.

Lonnie Reads Minds

MY FRIEND LONNIE WAS A PSYCHIC or a clairvoyant or whatever you call it when somebody reads minds. I was the first person he told. It was during the coming attractions to the new X-Men movie.

I offered Lonnie some of my popcorn and he took a handful. He looked like he had something on his mind and he said, "I do," and then he stuffed the popcorn in his mouth.

I said what was he planning to ask Andrea to marry him? Lonnie said no. He said actually he didn't know how much longer it was going to last with Andrea. Then he said what he meant was he had something on his mind. He said my thoughts were on his mind, and so were the thoughts of the two women sitting in front of us.

I said right, and then I pointed at the creepy looking guy sitting alone at the front of the theatre and asked Lonnie what he was thinking.

Lonnie said he didn't know. He said the guy was too far away, but if I wanted he could tell me what I was thinking. I said sure and then he did. A lot of it was pretty obvious, but he said it exactly like me, and some of the stuff wasn't so obvious, like the stuff about the girl at the coffee shop that afternoon. He even knew her hair colour and what way she was sitting and how she smiled at me and stuff.

I thought it was pretty cool, being able to read minds, but Lonnie said it wasn't. "It crams out everything else. I've tried to shut it off. I've tried earplugs, holding my breath, gritting my teeth, headphones. I've tried listening to all different types of music to see if there's one specific one that works and there isn't. I've started trying one note over and over, to see if there's a frequency or pitch that shuts it off, but so far nothing. It's horrible. I've completely lost track of what I think about stuff.

All I know is what other people think about stuff, and I can't even keep that straight."

He said that was why he didn't think it would last with Andrea. He said whenever they were alone and she was looking at him, she had all these doubts about whether or not she wanted to be with him, and meanwhile he didn't have a clue how he felt.

Lonnie kept on about it through the entire movie. The teenagers behind us kept going, "shhh." It got annoying and I wanted him to shut up, but he wouldn't. "I know you want me to shut up, but I need to talk about this," he said.

I asked Lonnie how long he'd been able to read minds, and he said a few months. He said he kept looking for something that might've triggered it, but he couldn't find it. He said the best he could come up with was the goldfish dying. "I flushed it down the toilet and then I went out and replaced it before Andrea came home. She doesn't say anything, but she knows and she's pissed off at me for it."

"Maybe it's nothing. Maybe it's just radio waves or something. You always hear about people who can get radio stations by touching their fillings together," I said.

"They don't do metal fillings anymore, and it doesn't work with enamel," Lonnie said.

Three months after that, Lonnie flipped out on Andrea. He accused her of thinking all these things she didn't say. He said she went pale when he did it, and then she started to cry, but she didn't deny any of it. She just packed up her things and left. He said she cried the whole time.

Six months after that, Lonnie jumped off a roof downtown. He jumped from so high up that they had to close the block off for four days while they fixed the street. He left a note about how he couldn't take hearing other people's thoughts anymore.

I tried to help Lonnie. I told him he needed to talk to other people about it. I suggested a psychiatrist, but Lonnie said no. He said he didn't want to lie on a couch and listen to someone else think about how crazy he was. "I've got to listen to you think it and that's enough," he said.

Lonnie finally told his mom, but she was pretty out of it, and Lonnie said she didn't get what he was saying, so Lonnie just kept bitching to me.

I'm seeing this woman now, Natalie. Things seem to be going well, like with Lonnie and Andrea. Sometimes I look at her, and I wonder what she's thinking, and I think Lonnie was just weak. I wouldn't mind being able to read people's minds. It'd be pretty useful a lot of the time.

Lonnie was too sensitive. Still, I shouldn't have thought that about him, at least not with him around. I don't even know if I meant it, but I lay awake at night and think about it. I mean I'd known the guy since we were kids. I just got so sick of listening to him complain.

The Straw That Broke the Camel's Back

THE NATIONAL RESEARCH COUNCIL in Canada looked into it and they determined that you couldn't break a camel's back with straw.

The goal of their research was to determine how many straws you would have to put on a camel's back in order to break it, and it turned out you couldn't physically pile that much straw onto a camel's back no matter how you packed it.

The National Research Council put out a press release saying that the straw was a false symbol, and that the phrase was entirely incorrect.

A dissenting researcher said maybe you couldn't break the back of a healthy camel with straw, but what about one that had been months on the Silk Road.

The whole argument is misguided. The truth about the straw and the camel's back isn't in scientific research. It's in an old Bedouin tale that was only translated into English in 2011.

There's just one English copy of the tale, and as far as anyone knows, there are only two copies in Arabic.

The story is about a raider who attacked caravans along the Silk Road. He'd come out of nowhere and he'd disappear back into nowhere.

The raider, whose name was Muqtar, always rode on horseback. The story has it that Muqtar – who rode with a small posse – had a magic straw and that when he put the straw on a camel's back, the camel's back would break. He and his posse would surround a convoy and then break the camels' backs. They'd make off with as much of the loot as they could, and of course, they couldn't be followed, because the convoy's camels all had broken backs.

Nobody took the story seriously. For one thing, the writing is awful, and for another, there's no moral. One day Muqtar and his posse just stop showing up to rob convoys.

In 2011 the story was translated into English by the US State Department, though. The State Department kept it very hush-hush, because some numb nuts "expert" on Arab history said he thought the Bedouin tale was a true story.

The crazy thing is that the numb nuts "expert" was right. Somehow he figured out from a line about an oasis with a U-shaped palm tree where Muqtar must have been based.

The US State Department hired a crew to dig where the "expert" said, and the crew uncovered sixteen guys buried in the sand. One of the sixteen guys had a straw in his pocket.

The State Department tested the straw and it turns out that the straw breaks camels' backs.

The State Department analysed the straw to figure out why it breaks camels' backs, and their hope is to create straws that will break the backs of other animals, including humans.

The feeling is that an intimate weapon like that is almost impossible to defend against. It doesn't make noise, it doesn't require skill, and it doesn't set off a metal detector.

Security is really tight on this. I know the State Department will deny everything I'm writing, and that probably no one will believe me, and if you ask my doctor, he'll say I broke my back falling off a ladder while I was cleaning out the eavestroughing, but ask yourself if that isn't quite the coincidence.

Dating Perfection

ANNIE AND I USED TO GO OUT. Annie was physically perfect. We started to suspect in high school, but I didn't go out with her until later. In grade eleven me and Faisal and Tim sat down in the cafeteria and tried to name somebody as perfect as Annie. We tried teachers, other students, movie stars, but there was nobody because Annie was perfect.

They actually proved it with a computer when we were twenty-two. MIT and Harvard did this massive study to see what people found attractive, and then they put together composites of what the perfect man and woman would look like. The composites didn't look slightly off like those things usually do. They were beautiful beyond belief, and the woman, she looked exactly like Annie. She was the same height and had the same body measurements. The perfect woman even had the same haircut Annie'd had in second year.

I went out with Annie for just over a year from when I was twenty-four. Annie asked me out. I never would have had the balls to ask out the perfect woman. My friends all thought it was bullshit that Annie was interested in me.

"How does a woman who's physically flawless wind up with Eddington here?" Faisal said and everyone else agreed.

I asked Annie once, and she said I wasn't so bad, but then she said that Aphrodite married Hephaestus, and Hephaestus was an ugly fucker covered in soot all the time. She also said she liked that I never told her I could see her inner beauty. She said all the guys she'd dated before told her that it was her inner beauty that they were really attracted to, but then they stared at her all the time and never listened to a word she said so fuck them.

Everybody gaped at Annie when they saw her. Even little kids who weren't interested in that sort of thing yet gaped.

In over a year of going out with Annie I never got over how she looked.

She told me once that being perfect depressed her. She said the people who did the study told her that she'd only be perfect until age twenty-six. They told her that after that it would be a slow decline. They told her that she'd probably be the most perfect woman in the world until age sixty-one, but she wouldn't be full on perfect after twenty-six.

Aside from being physically perfect, Annie was pretty normal. She wasn't stuck up at all about how she looked. She didn't spend all day at the gym or purge after meals or anything, but she was worried about what would happen when she wasn't perfect anymore.

They discovered Annie six months after they came out with the composites. They sent people all over the world to try and find the most perfect woman, but it was just some guy who saw her on the street and followed her home. They tried to make Annie famous, but she couldn't act and she couldn't sing and she was too chubby for modelling. Annie said she was happy with how it turned out, because she just wanted a normal life and she didn't want to be famous. They went looking for the perfect man too, but they didn't find him. The closest they came was a guy from Samoa who had the same eyes, but who otherwise didn't look much like the composite.

In just over a year, Annie and I never had sex. I told Faisal, and Faisal told Tim, and they sat me down and asked what was wrong with me. They said Jesus, did it not work or something? Tim said if I needed help, he could do it for me.

Faisal said how was Tim any better than me. He said it was obvious I was just a front, a nice guy to keep the assholes away. "Eddington's a cuckold. Look at him, it's Friday night and he's got Annie for a girlfriend but he's here with us. Annie's out with somebody else tonight," Faisal said.

I didn't tell them that I couldn't fuck perfection, that I'd tried, that we'd made out a couple of times and that I'd watched her masturbate, but I just couldn't bring myself to fuck her. I told my sister that, and she said I was just a pig who objectified women, but I still couldn't do it.

Annie broke up with me a week before she turned twenty-five. She said she couldn't take it anymore. She said she loved me. She said she wanted to fuck me and not somebody else, but she only had a year of being perfect left. She said she wasn't going to waste that when every guy she saw wanted her.

I told her they just thought they wanted her, that everybody thought they wanted her, but she was too perfect for any of them. "If you just had a flaw somewhere it would be easier. A cellulite deposit, a scar on your right cheek, something," I said.

Two weeks later Annie called me from the hospital. She'd cut her cheek open with a piece of glass from a wine bottle. The cut was pretty deep. The intern had to put in four stitches to close it up.

"Now you can fuck me," she said, but I still couldn't. Not that she wasn't still beautiful, but she gave up being perfect for me, and that made her human.

I don't care what anybody says. Nobody wants human. That's just what they settle for when they can't find perfection.

Writer's Block

THIS OLD GUY CAME INTO THE STORE with a package for a woman. I asked him how he wanted it sent, and he said he didn't want some fuck-up in a delivery truck who'd try three times to deliver it. He said he wanted me to deliver it in person, and then he gave me five hundred dollars and said I had a reliable face.

I said I wasn't a messenger boy, and he said of course, but I worked for a courier company, so surely I could courier this one package. He said he needed to make sure it got into her hands. I said if it was so important why didn't he do it, since it was just around the corner. He said if that was how I was going to be to give him his five hundred dollars back and he'd find somebody else, so I took the package.

I went to the woman's place after work. She had a condo on York. It was a nice place. The woman was about forty and she was pretty. I gave her the package, and she said what was it. I said I didn't know, that some guy had walked in and handed me the package and five hundred dollars to make sure it got to her.

The woman said that was creepy. She said sometimes it was creepy being famous. I told her I didn't know who she was, and she said she was a writer. She said probably it was some pervert sending her some lingerie or something. She said she had a guy once send her a pair of jeans and a note asking her to piss in them and send them back.

The woman said to stay put and then she went and got the scissors. She said probably it was some pervert, but if it wasn't and she was going to get blown up or be anthraxed or something, she didn't want to be alone.

I said what did I want to be blown up or anthraxed for, especially when it wasn't even about me, but I stood in the foyer with my shoes on while she opened the package. There was a little wooden block inside, painted blue. That was it.

"That's it?" she said and I shrugged. There was no return address on the package. She asked what the guy looked like, and I said a guy. I said about sixty, and in good shape. She said that wasn't helpful. She put the block on the mantle and I left.

I didn't think about it much after that, until I saw her six months later at Starbucks. She said hey. She said she was there to apply for a job. She said it was funny, but she hadn't written a word since two days before I brought her the package.

She said she didn't really know how to do anything except write, and now she couldn't seem to write, and she wasn't that famous that she wasn't stuck for cash if she couldn't write.

She mentioned the package and the block. I said I felt bad about that, and I was going to offer to take the block from her because I don't write and maybe the rule is that somebody has to take the block, you can't just get rid of it, but then she said not to feel bad. She said she loved the block. She said it was the most beautiful shade of blue and it was flawless. She said she'd measured it and it was a perfect cube and there wasn't a splinter anywhere. She said when she was stressed, especially about not being able to write, she'd take it off the mantle and caress it.

So I didn't offer to take the block off her hands. The woman had no imagination. What could she write that was worth reading?

Realism

THIS STORY IS ABOUT A GUY whose life is real. His life is more real than real life. It's life stripped down.

It started because people weren't buying life anymore. People said the emotions, the ideals, the advertising of life were all phoney, so they just got rid of them. They didn't put anything else in place of these things, so life became real.

The main character of this story is Dieter. Dieter is typical. His story is get up, shower, eat, ride the subway, get a coffee, work, eat lunch, work, get a doughnut, ride the subway, buy allergy medication, walk home, make dinner, eat, do the dishes, watch TV, go to bed and so on.

There's no conflict in Dieter's life, good or bad. The girl who gets Dieter his coffee doesn't make eyes at him, and the guy at the doughnut counter doesn't tell Dieter he's getting fat.

It's like that all around. Nobody has strong feelings about anything because strong feelings cause conflict, and because strong feelings are contrived and out of place and not like your life.

Dieter's day isn't always the same. He can do what he wants. Sometimes he skips the doughnut, and sometimes he goes down the street to the pub at lunch or after work and has a beer, and sometimes it rains and Dieter gets wet because he forgot his umbrella.

Dieter's day is never emotional, though. He doesn't have a lover, or even friends. He says hi, how are you, are you enjoying the weather, just the bill please, stuff like that, but that's it.

Dieter's life isn't dystopian. He doesn't lie awake at night wondering if his life is how it should be. There's no secret police around to drag off the couple fighting in the street so that nobody else sees them. The couple doesn't exist.

There's no teenage girl struggling to conform whose emotions, buried deep down, have the power to destroy the new social order, and there's no suppression of ideas and opinions.

This is just the story of Dieter as it is, and it's the story of reality, unvarnished.

The Council of Unfulfilled Dreams

MY DREAMS CAME INTO MY HOSPITAL ROOM after visiting hours. They piled in and grabbed a spot wherever, on the window sill, on the bed, hanging off the ceiling fan.

Every dream I'd ever had was there. I didn't even recognize most of them. There was one dream that was the spokesdream. It was from when I was seven or eight. I was on trial and Dracula was the judge.

The spokesdream said it was unfulfilled. It said they were all unfulfilled. I said great, but I was on my deathbed and what was I supposed to do about it.

The spokesdream said it was sorry for the timing. It said dreams are usually pretty passive and they'd discussed it in several committees, but anyway, they'd been concerned for some time now, and I was on my deathbed and it didn't look good.

I said visiting hours were over and they should go. I said the least they could do was hit me with this shit during daylight hours, but the dreams didn't leave. There was one dream about Napoleon riding through my elementary school that started to walk out, but it was stopped by a dream about being lost in a forest and another one about being the Soviet Premier.

The spokesdream said they were there to find fulfilment, or at least answers. It said they'd asked around with other dreams and it seemed like there were plenty of dreams being fulfilled, so why weren't any of them fulfilled. The spokesdream said it understood that dreams took their chances and that not all of them found fulfilment, but I could have made an effort to fulfil at least some of my dreams.

I said they were my dreams and it was up to me whether or not to fulfil them, and the spokesdream said what gave me that right. It said just because they were products of my imagination didn't mean I could abuse them. It said I couldn't do that to my children, why was it okay to do it to my dreams?

I said that was how it had always been, and the spokesdream said not anymore. It said they'd decided, and from now on they were going to be responsible for their own fulfilment. And then my dreams walked out on me and I had nothing.

The Possibilities Are Endless

THIS GUY MATSUMOTO PROVED that the possibilities aren't endless. It turns out there are a finite number of situations and a finite number of possibilities for each one. The number of possibilities is pretty huge, but the point is it's a number.

They've put the world's fastest computers on figuring out all the possibilities. At the current rate they should have all the possibilities mapped out in thirteen hundred years.

There's a possibility that the computers will get unplugged and the data will be lost and they'll have to start all over again. There's also the possibility that faster computers will take over and all the possibilities will be mapped out in ten years, or five even.

Once the computers are done, everyone can have access to all the possibilities. They'll be able to call them up on their phones so they can go through them all, and won't have to limit themselves to the couple of possibilities they can think of at that moment.

Industry leaders are working hard to make this a reality quickly. The thinking in industry is that there's a ton of money in giving people the possibilities.

Political leaders are encouraging industry, but for a different reason. They're afraid of choosing the wrong possibility and having people later, with all the possibilities at their fingertips, saying look at these two hundred pages of possibilities that would have been better than the one you chose.

So the politicians aren't doing anything except encouraging industry to figure out all the possibilities before they have to call elections.

Generally people are like the politicians. They're putting off making life decisions like having kids and buying houses. They're doing the basics. They're going to work and buying groceries and shit, but the entire developed world is in limbo waiting to see what the possibilities are.

They interviewed Matsumoto about it, and Matsumoto said that wasn't the point. He said the point was that it was theoretically possible to map out all the options. He said obviously this had been a possibility, but he hadn't considered it.

Life in Four Hours

THE COSMOS INTRODUCED its first major new technology in millennia: PVRs for people's lives. It's a big deal because it means that now you can skip all the boring shit that happens in your life: the transactions with the cashiers, the trips to the doctor, the standing in line. You can also cut out the awkward moments where everyone just looks at the ground and wishes they were somewhere else.

The PVRs have changed things a lot. They've opened up a ton of free time for people. The big new thing is to host a party where people come over and watch your life. You skip through to the highlights and you do your best to weave the scenes together with a voiceover.

Some people get arty with it. They throw in a shot of themselves at eight years old asleep in the suburbs in the summer with the window open and the crickets chirping. Some people have even showed their lives out of order. Most people stick to a pretty standard formula though, and it's just a question of how interesting their lives were and how self-indulgent they are.

Most people's lives boil down to something the length of The Godfather. Gone With the Wind is considered to be the upper limit for length unless you're really somebody important.

It's a long haul and most people have the sense to throw in an intermission somewhere between thirty and thirty-five. The majority live past seventy these days, but childhood is cuter and you do most of the really crazy shit when you're in your teens and twenties.

It's a much better way to live your life than the traditional way, and you can pause for a bathroom break any time you need to.

It has created problems though. The parties are very political, and you have to be careful who you invite, because the thing is, friends and family often have a different perspective on things than you do.

My friend Sammy, his sister invited her friends and family. It turned out that when she was nine, Sammy's sister stole her best friend's necklace, and Sammy's sister was also responsible for the rumours about her best friend's bedwetting in the seventh grade. Sammy's sister's friend held it in through the necklace, but when she found out about the bedwetting she lost it and she went after Sammy's sister right there in the den. Sammy's sister lost two teeth and ended up missing the rest of her life in a twenty-four hour dental surgery clinic.

Sammy went the other way. He didn't invite any of us. He went downtown and sold tickets for five bucks. He crammed three hundred strangers into his basement to watch his life. Now Sammy's mom won't talk to him.

Sammy told his mom that everyone needs secrets from their parents, but she didn't agree.

Even worse, she can actually watch Sammy's life any time she wants. One of the three hundred strangers brought a video camera and bootlegged Sammy's life. I found a copy of it for two bucks at Byward and George, and watched it one night with Sammy's sister. It turns out Sammy never even liked me. He tells a bunch of people that I'm just a friend by geography. He says he didn't even like me when we were kids, but he hung out with me because I had the only Commodore 64 in the neighbourhood and now he can't get rid of me.

He had some bad things to say about his sister too. His sister and I became an item after that. We made a point of dropping by Sammy's house when we knew he'd be home and we'd try to accidentally bump into him when he went places.

I still hadn't shown my life. One night we were talking, and Sammy and his sister said I should sell my PVR. "Even if you only get half your money back," Sammy said. "Just hole yourself up for the next eighty-six years the way people used to," his sister said.

I said that people didn't used to hole up for eighty-six years, and that that was the point. I said lives used to be a lot shorter and they happened non-stop, and nowadays there was so much dead time. I said I'd go nuts if I had to live my entire life from start to finish, and I didn't know how anyone could stand that.

That's pretty much how the marketing goes too. The slogan they use to sell the PVRs is: "You can't put a price on living. Your life. Your way."

In the end I did something different with my life. It's ninety-four minutes, all continuous. I'm thirty-seven. It starts with me walking down the street. I say hello to an old man at the corner and I turn to watch the ass of a teenage girl. I go to a coffee shop and I sit at a table with a woman I don't know. I say hi to the woman and we end up talking for an hour and it's the most amazing conversation about all sorts of things. After an hour, the woman gets up and leaves and I don't get her number or even her name.

I booked an auditorium for it and just threw the doors open. My hope was that this woman would come and that we could get to talking again. My friends and family are all pissed off because they're not in my life at all, except for a phone call from my mom that I don't answer. Sammy's sister was so mad about my life that she broke up with me.

She said it was obvious I still had a thing for the woman. She said I was so fucking transparent and my life was a disgusting display. Sammy was there when she broke up with me, and he had this big grin on his face, like finally I don't have to hang out with you anymore.

The woman wasn't at the screening, but she heard about it from a friend who was, and she got in touch with me. She asked me why I hadn't asked for her phone number, and then she asked me why I hadn't put a missed connection on Craigslist.

She said she'd been interested in me, but it was different, because we were alive then, and now she was seeing someone and it was pretty serious.

I got drunk after that and I smashed the PVR. Still, eighty-six years? Who has that kind of time to spend on life?

Sixty Minutes That Will Change Your Life

THERE WAS A POSTER ON A LAMPPOST for one of those conferences: sixty minutes that will change your life. The conference was only twenty bucks and my life wasn't so hot, so I went, and after my life was completely different.

There was a fat, grey-haired guy in a suit in charge of the whole thing. He talked for fifteen minutes about empowerment and stuff, and then his staff sat down with us and worked out a plan.

I got enrolled back in school, and I got a new part-time job that paid the same as I was already making, but in a third the hours. I got a new place down by the river and a dog and a girlfriend.

The guy said he'd like to see me in something long-term, but for now it was better if my girlfriend was just casual. My girlfriend was a year older than me and she had a Masters Degree and a good job and she was happy I was going back to school.

I was happy at first too, but school was a drag, because I was full-time and I also had the part-time job and the dog was just a puppy, and I hardly saw my girlfriend, and when I did she talked about her problems, which were different from mine.

I saw a poster outside the bathroom at Starbucks for another conference. This one was ninety minutes that would change my life. It cost a hundred dollars, which was a lot because I was a student, but I figured if twenty dollars had gotten me where I was, a hundred dollars would really do it.

The woman running the seminar was thin and had long dark hair and a shrill voice. She said we were there because we were dissatisfied. She said we didn't have to be dissatisfied. She said the next ninety minutes was about that, and then somebody went around and handed us portfolios. The woman said to read them over and she'd come around and we'd talk about them.

My portfolio had a new job that paid pretty well, and a house in the suburbs that I owned with a new girlfriend who wanted a family.

The woman came around and we talked. She asked me what I was doing and why, and I told her. She shook her head and said she never would have made me a student at my age. She said that was just sloppy.

She said she really liked my portfolio for me. She said the one change she'd like to make was to make it so my girlfriend was already pregnant. She said she could tell I'd be a good father. I said okay and off I went.

Life was good at first. We had a boy, and we got married, and our parents got along, and my buddy David gave a great speech at the wedding. As time went on the commute to work and the isolation of the suburbs got me down, though. I said I wanted to live in the city again, and my wife said the city was no place to raise a child.

I didn't like my job either. It seemed pointless. I looked around for other work, and I came across an ad for another conference. It was an evening that would change my life. The conference was ten thousand dollars, but it included dinner.

I told my wife about it, and she said what was wrong with our lives. Then she said those things were a scam anyway.

I went to the conference. The food was great, and a young couple in casual dress talked about how we all deserved to get the most out of life. The woman came and sat down with me during dessert and said she could see how I was marked out for something different.

She said she could tell I wasn't meant for that life, the endless commute, the worries about college and retirement. She said my mind was being wasted on those stresses.

I left the conference as a magnate. I had four girlfriends in three cities and my own plane and an army of people to do stuff for me.

It's really the life. I golf or swim or fuck, and I go to my office for a couple of hours a couple of times a week.

I've started my own seminars. They're priced depending on what you can afford. It's most of my business now, and I try to attend as many of them as I can.

There are people out there who say the seminars are a scam, and there are people out there who say they're happy with their lives and they don't want to change them, but they're just selling you a bill of goods. They're miserable and they want to keep you down. Don't let them. I went, and look at me now. Sixty minutes will change your life. Guaranteed.

Acknowledgements

In *The Big Picture*, I thanked everyone generally. This time, I would like to thank a few people specifically: Tara Dentry for being the first person to believe in my work; Nick Hamilton for being the first person to criticize my work; Myrna Rootham for her unwavering encouragement; Emma Jenkin for the fabulous cover art; Colin Richards for his technical expertise with the launch of *The Big Picture*, and the Words at the Wise reading series; Tamara Wise and the staff of Wise Bar for hosting us every month; Peter Jelen, my editor, for taking a chance on publishing *The Big Picture*, and for sticking with me through *Heaven's Gone to Hell*; all my family and friends for their love and support, especially Kaitlin Wainwright, without whom, who knows where I'd be.

About the Author

Andrew J. Simpson's work has appeared in various journals in Canada and internationally. He is a regular contributor to the *Feathertale Review*, and host of Toronto's sole fiction only reading series Words at the Wise. His first book, *The Big Picture,* is also available from *BareBackPress*. Learn more about what he's up to at http://versustheneanderthals.com.

Andrew J. Simpson

$18.99
6" x 9"
240 pages
ISBN-13: 978-0992035501
ISBN-10: 0992035503
BISAC: Fiction / General

I WALKED UP BEHIND GOD AND STUCK A SIGN ON HIS BACK. IT SAID "FREE WILL," OR "KICK ME."

The government is taxing your dreams and moments are being captured and held against their will. Murphy's Law is suspended pending the outcome of a constitutional challenge; a best-selling author writes and publishes the same novel fifteen times without anyone catching on, and all of humanity is put into receivership over a missing cup of coffee.

Andrew J. Simpson's debut anthology is a highly creative journey through the world of the surreally real. Savour the fantastical and the mundane, every nuance and notion that makes up The Big Picture.

www.ingramcontent.com/pod-product-compliance
Lightning Source LLC
Chambersburg PA
CBHW032120020726
47494CB00007BA/2163